THE EXPLOITS OF
MOOMINPAPPA

D1341486

Books by Tove Jansson

COMET IN MOOMINLAND

FINN FAMILY MOOMINTROLL

THE EXPLOITS OF MOOMINPAPPA

MOOMINSUMMER MADNESS

MOOMINLAND MIDWINTER

TALES FROM MOOMINVALLEY

MOOMINPAPPA AT SEA

MOOMINVALLEY IN NOVEMBER

Set down and illustrated by

Tove Jansson

THE EXPLOITS OF
MOOMINPAPPA

Described by Himself

Translated by Thomas Warburton

PUFFIN

PUFFIN BOOKS

Published by the Penguin Group
Penguin Books Ltd, 80 Strand, London WC2R ORL, England
Penguin Group (USA) Inc., 375 Hudson Street, New York, New York 10014, USA
Penguin Group (Canada), 90 Eglinton Avenue East, Suite 700, Toronto, Ontario, Canada M4P 2Y3
(a division of Pearson Penguin Canada Inc.)
Penguin Ireland, 25 St Stephen's Green, Dublin 2, Ireland
(a division of Penguin Books Ltd)
Penguin Group (Australia), 707 Collins Street, Melbourne, Victoria 3008, Australia
(a division of Pearson Australia Group Pty Ltd)
Penguin Books India Pvt Ltd, 11 Community Centre, Panchsheel Park, New Delhi – 110 017, India
Penguin Group (NZ), 67 Apollo Drive, Rosedale, Auckland 0632, New Zealand
(a division of Pearson New Zealand Ltd)
Penguin Books (South Africa) (Pty) Ltd, Block D, Rosebank Office Park, 181 Jan Smuts Avenue,
Parktown North, Gauteng 2193, South Africa

Penguin Books Ltd, Registered Offices: 80 Strand, London WC2R ORL, England

puffinbooks.com

First published in Finland as *Muminpappans Bravader* 1950
This translation published in England by Ernest Benn Ltd 1952
Published in Puffin Books 1969
This edition published 2012
001 – 10 9 8 7 6 5 4 3 2 1

The moral right of the author/illustrator has been asserted

Set in Plantin
Printed in Great Britain by Clays Ltd, St Ives plc

British Library Cataloguing in Publication Data
A CIP catalogue record for this book is available from the British Library

ISBN: 978-0-141-34533-8

www.greenpenguin.co.uk

MIX
Paper from
responsible sources
FSC
www.fsc.org   FSC™ C018179

Penguin Books is committed to a sustainable
future for our business, our readers and our planet.
This book is made from Forest Stewardship
Council™ certified paper.

ALWAYS LEARNING   **PEARSON**

CONTENTS

PREFACE   7

CHAPTER 1   9
*In which I tell of my misunderstood childhood,
of the tremendous night of my escape, of the
building of my first Moominhouse, and of my
historical meeting with Hodgkins.*

CHAPTER 2   23
*Introducing the Muddler and the Joxter, and
presenting a spirited account of the construction
and matchless launching of the houseboat.*

CHAPTER 3   37
*Recapitulating my first heroic exploit, its stag-
gering outcome, a few thoughts, and my first
confrontation with the Niblings.*

CHAPTER 4   56
*In which the description of my Ocean voyage
culminates in a magnificent tempest and ends in
a terrible surprise.*

CHAPTER 5   68

In which (besides giving a little specimen of my intellectual powers), I describe the Mymble family and the Surprise Party which brought me some bewitching tokens of honour from the hand of the Autocrat.

CHAPTER 6   85

In which I become a Royal Outlaw Colonist and show remarkable presence of mind when meeting the Ghost of Horror Island.

CHAPTER 7   100

Describing the triumphant unveiling of the Amphibian and its sensational trial dive to the bottom of the sea.

CHAPTER 8   112

In which I give an account of the circumstances of the Muddler's wedding, further touch on the dramatic night when I first met Moomin-mamma, and finally write the remarkable closing words of my Memoirs.

EPILOGUE   127

MOOMIN-GALLERY   132

PREFACE

I, MOOMINPAPPA, am sitting tonight by my window gazing into my garden, where the fireflies embroider their mysterious signs on the velvet dark. Perishable flourishes of a short but happy life!

As a father of a family and owner of a house I look with sadness on the stormy youth I am about to describe. I feel a tremble of hesitation in my paw as I poise my memoir-pen.

Still, I draw strength from some words of wisdom I have come across in the memoirs of another remarkable personage: 'Everyone, of whatever walk in life, who has achieved anything good in this world, or thinks he has, should, if he be truth-loving and nice, write about his life, albeit not starting before the age of forty!'

I feel rather nice, and I like truth when it isn't too boring. I will attain the suitable age on 9 August.

Yes, I really think I must yield to Moomintroll's persuasion and to the temptation of talking about myself, of getting into print and being read all over Moominvalley! May my simple notes bring delight and instruction to all Moomins, and especially to my dear son, even if my memory isn't quite what it has been.

And you, foolish little child, who think your father a dignified and serious person, when you read this story of three daddies' adventures you should bear in mind that one daddy is very like another (at least when young).

I believe many of my readers will thoughtfully lift their snout from the pages of this book every once in a while to exclaim: 'What a Moomin!' or: 'This indeed is life!'

Last but not least I want to express my heartfelt thanks to the people who most of all contributed to forming my life into the work of art it has become: Hodgkins, the Hattifatteners, and my wife, the matchless and exceptional Moominmamma.

Moominvalley in August

CHAPTER I

In which I tell of my misunderstood childhood, of the tremendous night of my escape, of the building of my first Moominhouse, and of my historical meeting with Hodgkins.

ONE cold and windy autumn evening many years ago a newspaper parcel was found on the doorstep of the Home for Moomin Foundlings.

In that parcel I lay, quite small and shivering with cold, and without the least idea of where my father and mother were. (I've thought sometimes how much more romantic it would have been if mother had only laid me instead on green moss, in a small straw basket. But she probably hadn't any.)

The Hemulen who had built the Foundlings' Home snorted her customary snort and clamped a numbered seal on my tail to avoid mixing me up with the other Moominchildren. There were a lot of us, and we all soon became grave and tidy youngsters, because the Hemulen had a most solid character and used to wash us more often than she kissed us.

Still, she had one little weakness; she was interested in astrology, and every time a Moominchild was found on her doorstep she observed the position of the stars. They seem to be most important things!

Just imagine – had I come into the world only half an hour later I would have felt compelled to join the Hemulic Voluntary Brass Band, and one day earlier only gamblers were born. (Mothers and fathers should keep such things well in mind.)

But when the Hemulen looked at my stars she just shook her head and exclaimed: 'This will be no easy Moomin. He's overtalented.'

I think she was right (except that I have always felt at ease with myself).

I'll never forget the house we lived in. It wasn't like a Moominhouse at all. No surprising nooks and corners, no secret chambers, no stairs, no balconies, no towers. The Foundlings' Home was bleak and square, and it stood on a lonely heath.

I remember the fog, and the cries of the night birds, and the lonely trees on the horizon – and dark corridors with rows and rows of doors opening on square and beery-brown rooms. I remember that nobody was ever allowed to eat treacle sandwiches in bed or to keep pets under it, or to get up at night for a walk and chat.

I remember the dismal smell of oatmeal soup. And just imagine that you had to carry your tail at a certain angle when saying 'good morning' to the Hemulen!

'Have you washed your ears?' she inquired. 'Whatever are you thinking of?' she asked. 'Please be sensible!' she said.

I wasn't sensible. At first I was only unhappy.

I used to stand before the mirror and look deep in my unhappy eyes and heave sighs such as: 'Oh, cruel fate!'

'Oh, terrible lot.' 'Nevermore.' And in a few minutes I
felt a little better.

But then spring came . . .
It came all at once. Shoots and sprouts pushed dazedly
out of the ground, crumpled like the ears of new-born
Moominchildren. New winds were singing at night, and
the world was full of all kinds of whirring, chirping, and
humming noises. Everything was new once again.

And one day I heard a calm, regular thunder far away.
The sea had shed its ice, and the surf was breaking
on the shore. But we were never allowed to go to the
shore.

I walked about, all alone, thinking.

I thought of everything I've just described to you. Of
stars, Hemulens, square rooms, tail-seals, and the surf.
And I expect you'll understand that I decided to run away.
There simply wasn't anything else to do.

The escape was easy, almost too easy.

I had only to wait until everybody was asleep. Then I silently opened my window and made fast the Hemulen's clothes-line to the ledge. Very silently I slipped down to the wet ground and stood there listening. The surf was there as before, and so were all the night sounds. I had never heard them more clearly.

But before I left I laid a letter on the same doorstep where I had once been found in a newspaper parcel. It read:

Dear Hemulen,

I feel great events awaiting me. Life is short, the world is enormous. Perhaps I shall return one day decked in laurel wreaths. So long, and all best wishes from

A Moomin who is unlike others.

PS. I'm taking a pot of pumpkin mash with me.

I'm still of the opinion that it was a good letter, deeply and strongly worded. I expect the Hemulen's conscience gave her a good pinch.

And so I went. Straight into the night, all alone and a little afraid – but not much. I think.

*

At this point in his Memoirs Moominpappa was very deeply moved by the tale of his unhappy childhood, and he felt that he needed a rest. He screwed the top on his memoir-pen and went over to the window. All was silent in the Valley of the Moomins.

A light breeze was whispering in the silver poplars and gently swinging Moomintroll's rope ladder to and fro. 'I'm sure I'd manage an escape still if I needed to,' Moomin-pappa thought. 'Who cares if I'm not as young as I used to be!'

He chuckled to himself. Then he lowered his slightly rheumatic legs over the window ledge and reached for the rope ladder.

It swung about and he had great difficulty in keeping his balance.

'Drat the thing,' said Moominpappa softly, beginning to feel giddy.

'Hullo, Father,' said Moomintroll at the next window. 'What are you up to?'

'Exercises, my boy,' answered Moominpappa. 'Keeping fit! One step down, two up, one down, two up. Good for the muscles.'

'Better be careful,' said Moomintroll. 'How are the Memoirs going?'

'Very well,' answered Moominpappa and hauled his trembling legs into safety over the window ledge. 'I've just run away. The Hemulen cries with grief. I think it will be very moving.'

'When are you going to read it to us?'

'Soon. As soon as I'm sure it's going to be a best-seller. Bring Sniff and Snufkin the day after tomorrow to hear the first chapter. There's nothing more pleasant than reading your own book aloud!'

'I suppose not,' said Moomintroll and stifled a yawn. 'Well, good night, Father!'

'G'night, Moomintroll,' answered Moominpappa, already unscrewing the top of his memoir-pen.

*

Well. Where was I . . . Oh yes, I had run away, and then in the morning – no, that was a little later.

All the night I wandered through that strange and gloomy country. I didn't dare stop to rest; I didn't even dare look around me. I might have caught sight of something in the darkness! Sometimes I tried to whistle, to show myself that it wasn't so bad. But my voice trembled so much that it only frightened me all the more. But as for going back – never in the world! Not after such an imposing letter of farewell.

And finally the misty night came to an end. When the sun rose something very beautiful happened. The first bunches of sunlight suddenly made the mist as rosy-red as the veil on the Hemulen's Sunday bonnet. In a moment the whole world became pink and friendly-looking!

I halted and saw the night dissolve itself in thin glowing veils. Cobwebs and wet leaves were heavy with glistening rubies. My heart turned a somersault for pure happiness. Ho! I tore the hateful seal from my tail and threw it far away among the heather. And there and then I danced the Moomin dance of dawning freedom in the dewy and glistening spring morning, with my nice small ears pucked and my snout lifted against the sky.

No more washing by others' orders! No more eating just because it was dinner-time! No more saluting *anybody* other than a King (I'm a staunch royalist, in case you didn't know), and no more sleeping in square, beery-brown coloured rooms! Triumph!

First of all I ate the pumpkin mash and tossed the pot away. Now I had nothing to call my own. I knew nothing, but believed a lot. I did nothing by habit. I was extremely happy.

And I walked and walked and walked along the winding and wriggling path, and once more evening came, and then it was night again with a wind and a gale.

The night was black as pitch; I heard rustling and crackling all about me, and great wings went whispering and swishing over my head. The ground became uneven and soft, and I lost the path. A strange and nice smell filled the air and my snout with expectation. I didn't know yet that it was the wood's perfume of moss, bracken, and wet leaves. I felt very tired when I curled up and tried to warm my cold paws against my stomach. The great orchestra of the gale played overhead, and in the moment I went to sleep I thought: 'Tomorrow!'

When I awoke I lay on my back looking straight up into a world of green and gold and white. The trees around me were tall and strong pillars that lifted their green roof to a dizzying height. The leaves swayed gently and glittered in the morning light, and a lot of birds were dashing, giddy with delight, through the shafts of sun. Gleaming white honeysuckle hung everywhere in bunches and curtains from the branches. Gold and green and white! I stood on my head for a moment to calm myself.

Then I shouted:

'Hello! Who does this place belong to?'

'Don't bother us! We're busy playing!' the birds screeched back.

I went farther into the wood. In the shade of the giant bracken there were swarms of small creatures jumping and flying about. But they were too small to understand serious conversation.

At last I met a hedgehog who was busy polishing a large nutshell.

'Good morning, ma'am,' I said. 'I'm a lonely refugee who was born under rather special stars.'

'Really,' said the hedgehog, not too enthusiastically. 'Pretty shell, isn't it? It's going to be a milk-bowl.'

'Very pretty,' I said. 'Who owns this place?'

'Why, nobody! Or everybody, I suppose,' said the hedgehog.

She seemed surprised.

'Me, too?' I asked.

'By all means,' said the hedgehog and continued her polishing.

'Are you quite sure that it doesn't belong to some Hemulen or other?' I asked, a little worriedly.

'Hemulen?' said the hedgehog. 'What's that?'

'A Hemulen reaches almost double the height of ordinary bracken,' I explained. 'Snout protruding and slightly depressed. Pink eyes. No ears, but instead a couple of tufts of ginger-coloured or blue hair. The Hemulen isn't outstandingly intelligent and easily becomes a fanatic. Her feet are terribly large and flat. She cannot learn to whistle, and so dislikes all whistling. She . . .'

'Oh, good gracious,' said the hedgehog and backed away among the bushes.

'Well,' I thought. 'Probably they have no Hemulens here. Nobody's place and everybody's place. Mine, too. What shall I do?'

The idea came to me all at once, as is usually the case. (I just hear a faint 'click', and there it is.) Given a Moomin and a place, and there must follow a house. I was going to build a house with my own hands, a house exclusively my own!

I built it by the brook, where the grass was green and soft and exactly suitable for a Moomin-garden. All around it dense thickets stood in full bloom, trailing their boughs in the water.

My first Moominhouse arose with mysterious speed. That must have been due to inherited ability, but also to talent, good judgement and a sure taste. But one mustn't indulge in self-praise, so I'll only give you a simple sketch of the result.

It was quite a small house, but tall and slender as a Moominhouse should be, and adorned with several balconies, stairs, and turrets. The hedgehog lent me a fret-saw to do the pine-cone pattern on the verandah balustrade. As for the porch, I had to leave out the brass doors, of course, but even without them my house unmistakably resembled a porcelain stove of the genuine old kind. (You see, we Moomins always try to preserve the style from old times, when we used to live behind porcelain stoves. That was before central heating.) And when it was finished I went downstairs again feeling very contented. It was a kind of last farewell to the Hemulen.

But after a while I discovered that I was feeling slightly bored in some strange way. This surprised me and even made me angry with myself. But there it was. And believe

me, boredom when you ought to enjoy yourself is the worst kind of boredom.

I went and called on the hedgehog.

'Well?' she said. 'Only don't say a word about Hemulens.'

'No, no,' I said. 'But won't you come and look at my house? We could sit there for a while and have a chat. I'll tell you all about my strange birth.'

'That would be fascinating,' said the hedgehog. 'I'm so sorry I haven't got the time. I'm making milk-bowls for all my daughters.'

And that went for all the people in the wood. The birds, the worms, the tree-spirits, and the mousewives seemed to be in a great hurry about something or other. Nobody wanted to look at my house, or hear about my escape, or about the strange way I came into the world.

I went back to my green garden by the brook and sat down on the verandah. My verandah. My lonely fretwork verandah.

And suddenly – click – I had a new idea: to find out where the brook led.

I stepped into the cool water and began wading downstream. The brook ran as brooks do; with many freaks and

no hurry. Sometimes it rippled along, clear and shallow, over lots and lots of pebbles, and sometimes the water darkened and rose up to my snout. There were blue and red water-lilies floating everywhere in the stream. The sun was already setting and shone straight in my face. And after a while I began to feel almost happy again.

Then I heard a funny little whirring noise. Straight in front of me a splendid water-wheel was spinning. It was made of small sticks and stiff palm-leaves.

And somebody said: 'Please be careful.'

I looked up and saw a couple of hairy ears in the long grass by the brook.

'I'm just looking,' I said. 'Who are you?'

'Hodgkins,' said the owner of the ears. 'And you?'

'The Moomin,' I said. 'A lonely refugee born under rather special stars.'

'What stars?' asked Hodgkins, and his question made me very happy, because it was the first time anybody had asked me something I wanted to answer.

So I went to the shore and sat down at his side, and there I told him everything that had happened to me since the day I was found in the newspaper parcel. (Only I told him it had been a small basket of leaves.) And all the time the water-wheel was spinning in a little cloud of glittering waterdrops, and the sun reddened and sank, and my heart found new peace and happiness.

'Strange,' said Hodgkins when I had finished. 'Rather strange. That Hemulen. Bit of a cad, I think.'

'Quite,' I said.

'Not many worse, are there?' said Hodgkins.

'Certainly not,' I said.

Then we were silent for a while and looked at the sunset.

It was Hodgkins who showed me how to construct a water-wheel, an art that I have later taught my son. (Cut two forked branches and stick firmly in stream. Sandy bottom is best. Choose four stiff leaves, cross to form a star, pierce with stick. Strengthen construction with twigs. Carefully place stick on forks, and wheel will turn.)

In the evening twilight Hodgkins and I walked back to my house and I asked him in.

He said it was a good house. (Thereby he meant that it

was a wonderful and fascinating house. Hodgkins never cared much for big words.) The night wind came and sang us a song.

I had now found my first friend, and so my life was truly begun.

CHAPTER 2

Introducing the Muddler and the Joxter, and presenting a spirited account of the construction and matchless launching of the houseboat.

WHEN I awoke the following morning Hodgkins was already casting a net in the brook.

'Hello,' I said. 'Any fish here?'

'Hardly,' said Hodgkins. 'Still, we might catch something else. Want to come and meet the Muddler?'

We locked the door and went.

The Muddler lived quite near. He was very small and muddly, Hodgkins told me, and he had made himself at home in an American coffee tin; the blue kind.

'Is he a relative of yours?' I asked.

'My nephew,' Hodgkins said. 'Adopted him. Father and mother disappeared in a spring-cleaning.'

'How terrible,' I said. 'Were they never found?'

'Never,' Hodgkins answered.

He took out his cedarwood whistle that had a pea inside, and whistled twice.

The Muddler came running at breakneck speed, trying

23

to beat his tail and flap his ears and whisk his whiskers at the same time.

'Evening!' he cried. 'Why, that's grand! Whom are you bringing? Gee, what an honour! Excuse me please, things are a bit upside-down in my tin, but if you'd just ...'

'Never mind,' Hodgkins said. 'We're just out for a walk. Want to come along?'

'Why, sure!' the Muddler cried. 'Just a minute, please, I'll have to bring a few things along ...'

And he disappeared inside his tin where we heard him start a terrific rummaging. After a while he came out again carrying a wooden box under his arm, and so we all walked along together through the wood.

'Dear nephew,' Hodgkins suddenly said. 'Can you paint?'

'Can I paint!' exclaimed the Muddler. 'Sure, I've painted portraits of all my cousins! A separate portrait of each and every one! Excuse me, do you need some extra special, A-1 de-luxe painting done?'

'You'll see. It's a secret so far,' Hodgkins answered.

At that the Muddler became so excited that he started jumping about on his toes, and the string around his box snapped, and out tumbled a heap of his personal belongings, such as wire springs, paper clips, ear-rings, tins, dried frogs, cheese-knives, trouser-buttons, and pipe-cleaners, among other things.

'Well, well,' said Hodgkins and helped him to collect it all again.

'I had a really dandy piece of string once, only I lost it somewhere! Excuse me!' the Muddler said.

Hodgkins produced a strong length of rope and tied it around the box, and so we walked on again.

Finally, he halted by a large fig thicket and said:

'Enter, please.'

We made our way through the green bushes, stopped, turned our heads upwards, and exclaimed respectfully: 'A ship!'

It looked large and deep and strong, and its blunt stem disappeared out of sight somewhere in the shadows of the thicket.

'My houseboat,' Hodgkins said.

'Your what?' I asked.

'Houseboat,' Hodgkins repeated. 'A house built aboard a boat. Or a boat built beneath a house. You live aboard. Nice and practical.'

'And where's the house?' I asked.

Hodgkins let his paw describe a sweeping gesture. 'Your house by the brook,' he said.

'Hodgkins,' I replied, feeling a catch in my throat, 'when our mutual talents are joined there'll be no limit to their scope.'

By this time the Muddler had regained his breath and

was able to shout: 'Gee, is it really true? Oh! May I paint that ship? Cross your heart?'

'Cross my heart, yes. Choose your own colour,' Hodgkins replied. 'But be careful about the water-line. And her name is *The Ocean Orchestra*. That's the title of my long-lost brother's book of poems. You'll have to paint the name marine blue.'

Glorious times! Immortal deeds! Triumphantly we marched back to my house and began moving it to the shipyard. 'Grab hold now,' said Hodgkins. 'Easy does it. ... Raise a bit more on that side! Now she moves ...'

'Careful with the verandah, please!' I cried.

'Excuse me! The cellar got on my toes!' shouted the Muddler. And as he said it the house tipped up and a person came tumbling out of an upper window.

We looked at him.

'Hello!' I said threateningly.

'Hello yourself,' said the Joxter (for it was he).

'Why did you enter my house?' I continued.

HODGKINS' LOST BROTHER

The Joxter took his pipe from his mouth and explained genially: 'Because you had locked the door.'

'Sure, that's him all over!' cried the Muddler. 'He likes everything you mustn't do. He's always fighting policemen and laws and traffic signs.'

'And park keepers,' completed the Joxter. 'Has anybody had any breakfast yet?'

'No, quite the contrary,' said Hodgkins. 'Nephew! That pudding. Anything left?'

'Sure,' said the Muddler. 'Seen it yesterday. . . . Of course, my house is small and unworthy – but still – if I run along now and tidy it up a bit . . .'

And the Muddler clutched his box tightly under his arm and rushed off.

'Somebody hold the verandah,' said Hodgkins. 'I think we'll manage. We'll take the boathouse to the houseboat and have breakfast afterwards.'

'Isn't the Joxter going to help?' I asked (because I was still a little cross with him).

'Born lazy,' explained Hodgkins. 'Has to be forbidden to lend a hand. Then does it. Possibly.'

And then the auxiliary engine wouldn't work. The paddles refused to turn the screw, and not even my mind was able to cope successfully with the problem. (My modesty compels me to admit that there are three fields where my genius appears to feel somewhat cramped, namely, engineering, mathematics, and cookery.)

The Muddler had fried us an omelette, because he had lost the pudding somewhere.

'O.K.?' he asked anxiously and looked at Hodgkins.

Hodgkins was chewing most carefully with a strange look on his face. Finally he said: 'These knobbly things. Stuffing, what?'

'Knobbly things!' cried the Muddler. 'That must be something from my collection. Spit them out, please!'

Hodgkins deposited them on his plate. They were black and bevelled and prickly.

'Oh, *please* excuse me!' cried the Muddler. 'It's my cogwheels. What luck you didn't swallow them!'

But Hodgkins didn't answer him. He frowned deeply and sat looking down at his plate.

Then the Muddler started to cry.

'Hodgkins, you'll have to forgive the Muddler,' said the Joxter. 'Can't you see that he's really sorry?'

'Forgive him?' said Hodgkins. 'My nephew has earned a medal.' And he produced a pencil and some paper and showed us where the bevelled cogwheels would make the screw turn. He drew it like this:

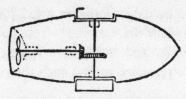

(I saw the point at once, but the others had to study it for a while.)

'You don't mean that you need *my* cogwheels for your invention?' cried the Muddler blissfully. 'Then I've almost built the auxiliary engine myself!'

The Muddler was so inspired by this that he donned his largest pinafore and started to paint *The Ocean Orchestra* at once. He painted with all his might. The houseboat was quite red when he had finished, and so was the ground, and most of the shipyard, too; and never in my life have I seen anything redder than the Muddler himself.

When it was all finished Hodgkins came for an inspection.

'Isn't it beautiful?' the Muddler said nervously. 'I've worked very carefully.'

Hodgkins looked at the water-line and said: 'Mphm.' Then he looked at the name on the prow and said: 'Mphm, mphm.'

'Is the spelling wrong?' asked the Muddler. 'Please say something or else I shall start crying again. Excuse me! It wasn't an easy name!'

'The O s h u n, O x t r a,' spelled Hodgkins. 'Well. Well, well. Oh, yes. And why not? The water-line ... I suppose the waves will fit in quite nicely. I see there's some paint left. Keep it.'

Then the Muddler was happy again and rushed away to paint his house.

And in the evening Hodgkins tried his net in the brook. And what did he find? You couldn't guess. A small binnacle, and inside it a brand new aneroid barometer! How strange to find such things in our little brook!

*

'Strange indeed,' said Moomintroll. He lay on his back beneath the lilac bushes looking at the bumblebees.

'Father,' he continued. 'Is it really quite true, all that you have written? Every word?'

'Every single word of it, my boy,' Moominpappa replied solemnly. 'I may have *stressed* some of the events a little, but that's only to make them more convincing.'

'I wonder what became of my father's collection,' Sniff said.

'Eh?' said Moomintroll.

'Father's button collection,' Sniff said. 'The Muddler was my father, wasn't he?'

'Certainly,' replied Moominpappa.

'Well, then, I'm just wondering,' Sniff said. 'I ought to have inherited it.'

'And what became of *my* father?' asked Snufkin.

'The Joxter?' said Moominpappa. 'Well, children, one doesn't always know what happens to daddies ... or to their collections. Still, I have saved yours for posterity by writing about them.'

'He didn't like park keepers either,' mumbled Snufkin. 'Just think of that ...'

They all stretched out their legs in the grass and lazily flapped their ears to drive the flies away. The weather was nice and sleepy.

'Have you written any more of it?' asked Moomintroll.

'Not yet,' replied Moominpappa. 'But if you can keep quiet now I'll finish the chapter and read it to you after dinner. Where's my memoir-pen?'

'Here,' said Snufkin. 'Please promise that you'll write the full truth and nothing but the truth about the Joxter! Even if he gets nabbed by the police.'

'I promise,' said Moominpappa, and continued his writing.

*

The day of the launching was unusually warm. Wonderful to behold *The Oshun Oxtra* resting in the shipyard on its

31

four rubber wheels (for climbing sand banks), and on the roof of the boathouse shone a gilded knob.

'So you're moving again,' said the Joxter and yawned. 'What a life! No end of changing and building-up and pulling down again and jumping about. Such a lot of work may turn out to be really harmful. Oh, I'm dejected just to think of all the people who work and buzz and bumble about, and of what it all leads to. I had a cousin once who studied trigonometry until his whiskers drooped, and when he had learnt it all a Groke came and ate him up. When do we start?'

'Are you coming, too?' I asked.

'Of course!' said the Joxter in an astonished voice.

'Please excuse me,' said the Muddler, 'but as it happens I had also something like that in mind ... I can't bear to live in my coffee tin any longer.'

'No?' I said.

'That red paint never dries!' explained the Muddler. 'Excuse me! It gets in my food and in the bed and in my whiskers. I'm going plumb crazy, Hodgkins, plumb crazy!'

'By all means don't,' said Hodgkins. 'Go and pack. Because we are launching *The Oshun Oxtra* today.'

'Gee!' cried the Muddler. 'Dear me, I have lots and lots to do! Such a long journey ... such a new life. ...' And the Muddler rushed off spattering paint in all directions.

But the launching gave us much to think about. The wheels of the houseboat were sunk deep in the moss, and the mast was hopelessly stuck in the fig thicket.

We dug up the ground. We pulled down the shipyard. Still *The Oshun Oxtra* didn't move.

Hodgkins sat down and put his head in his paws.

'Don't grieve. We'll find a way,' I said.

'I'm not grieving. I'm thinking,' replied Hodgkins soberly. 'This is the problem. A ship is stuck. Un-movable. You can't push it in the river. Then the river must be pushed to the ship. How? You change its course. How? You damn it up. How? You pile stones in it.'

'How?' I asked.

'NO!' Hodgkins exclaimed with a force that made me jump. 'No stones. Edward the Booble. Sits down in the river. Fills it up. Makes a dam.'

'Is his behind so big?' I asked.

'Bigger,' Hodgkins said. 'Biggest animal in the world. Next to his brother. Have you a calendar?'

'No,' I said, beginning to feel excited.

'Pea-soup, day before yesterday.* Bathing-day today†,' mused Hodgkins. 'All clear then. Come along, Moomin.'

'Are Boobles nice?' I asked carefully as we walked along down the river beach.

'Not very. But not dangerous either,' said Hodgkins. 'Tread on you only by mistake. Then weep for a week afterwards. And pay for the funeral too.'

'No great help, that,' I said, feeling rather brave (for if you're not afraid how can you be really brave?).

'Here he is,' said Hodgkins suddenly.

'Where?' I said. 'Does he live in this tower?'

'No tower. It's his leg,' replied Hodgkins. 'Keep quiet now, please. I'll have to shout.'

And then he shouted at the top of his voice: 'Ahoy, up there! Hodgkins down here! Mr Edward, where are you bathing this fine day?'

---

* All Boobles have pea-soup on Thursdays.
† All Boobles take a *special* bath on Saturdays.

'In the sea, of course, you sand flea,' replied a thunder somewhere in the sky.

'In the river! Running water! Excellent sand bottom!' roared Hodgkins.

'Lies and trumpery,' said Edward the Booble. 'Every mouseling knows the river is all full of stones.'

'No, no! Nice and smooth!' shouted Hodgkins back.

The Booble grumbled like a faraway thunderstorm. Then he said: 'All right. I'll bathe in the river. Get out of my way, I haven't the money for any more funerals. And if you've tricked me you'll have to pay for it yourself. You know I have such sensitive feet.'

'Now!' Hodgkins panted when we went running back. 'He'll sit down ... in the river ... angry ... the water will rise ... flooding the wood ... and ...'

'Here it comes!' I shouted, hearing a great splash in the distance.

We almost stumbled over the Joxter, who had curled himself up peacefully in the tool chest.

'All aboard!' cried Hodgkins. 'Sleeping on my tools, indeed!'

And no sooner had we lifted our tails inside the railing

when the flood wave reached our houseboat. In a whirling cascade of white foam *The Oshun Oxtra* was carried free from all its entanglements and was ploughing along through the wood. The paddles swished, the screw turned. The Muddler's cogs were functioning perfectly.

With a steady paw Hodgkins took the helm and steered us safely between the trees.

What a matchless launching! Blossoms and leaves were raining over the deck, splendidly adorning *The Oshun Oxtra* for its final triumphant leap into the river.

With happily splashing paddles she swept out into the middle of the stream. The gilded knob high on the roof gleamed and shone in the sun.

'Look out for sand banks,' shouted Hodgkins. 'I want to try one. To test the hinge-and-wheel construction.'

I looked out over the river, but all I saw was some sort of red tin bobbing on the waves some distance ahead.

'Just a tin,' I reported.

35

'That reminds me,' said the Joxter. 'There might be some kind of a Muddler in it.'

'You have forgotten your nephew!' I said to Hodgkins.

'Indeed, how could I?' he replied.

Soon we saw the Muddler's red face appearing over the rim of the tin. He flapped his arms and ears wildly and was obviously in danger of strangling himself in his scarf.

The Joxter and I leaned over the railing and took hold of the tin. It was still quite sticky with paint and rather heavy.

'Mind the deck,' said Hodgkins when we hoisted the tin aboard. 'How do you feel, dear nephew?'

'I'm going crazy!' said the Muddler. 'Think of it! Waves flooding into my packing. . . . Everything downside-up! I've lost my best window-catch and probably the pipe-cleaner, too. My nerves are all unsorted and so is my collection.'

And the Muddler began happily to arrange his collection anew. *The Oshun Oxtra* continued its journey, peacefully gliding and mildly splashing along down the river. I said to Hodgkins:

'I hope we'll see no more of Edward the Booble. Do you think he's very angry with us by now?'

'Rather,' replied Hodgkins, lighting his pipe.

CHAPTER 3

Recapitulating my first heroic exploit, its staggering out-come, a few thoughts, and my first confrontation with the Niblings.

W E left the green and friendly woods behind us. Now everything became large and gloomy. Strange animals wandered bellowing and sneezing along the steep river banks. We were lucky to have Hodgkins at the helm, be-cause the Joxter never took anything seriously, and the Muddler's main interest always circled around his tin. We had put it on the foredeck, and it was slowly drying in the sunshine. (But we never quite succeeded in cleaning up the Muddler himself; he remained slightly pink.)

Most of the time I sat in the steering cabin, looking at the unknown country, tapping at the aneroid barometer, or taking a little exercise on the verandah that served as the captain's bridge.

One evening we made our course into a deep and lonely bay.

'I don't like this place,' remarked the Joxter. 'It gives me Forebodings.'

'I dunno,' Hodgkins said. 'Good anchorage. Nephew! Cast the anchor, will you?'

'Aye, aye, sir. At once, sir,' cried the Muddler, and promptly tossed our kettle overboard.

'Did it have our supper in it?' I asked.

'I'm afraid it did,' said the Muddler dejectedly. 'Excuse me! So easy to grab the wrong thing. I'll make you some jelly instead . . . where's my sugar?'

'In the shoe-box,' said Hodgkins, and let the anchor down himself. 'What's up, Joxter?'

'I thought I heard something,' the Joxter mumbled. He stood at the railing and looked at the shore with gleaming eyes. Dusk was falling over the mountains that stretched, row after row, to the horizon.

'Hush!' said the Joxter. 'I heard it again.'

We all cocked our ears.

'You must have been mistaken,' I said. 'Come along inside, I'm going to light the kerosene lamp.'

'Here's the jelly,' said the Muddler, and jumped out of his tin with a dish in both hands.

Then we all heard it.

A howl and a wail, a hunting call far away in the mountains. The Muddler cried out and dropped his dish with a crash.

'That's the Groke,' said Hodgkins.

'Can she swim?' I asked.

'Don't know,' said Hodgkins. 'Listen, she's out for somebody.'

The Groke was hunting in the mountains. She howled horribly – sometimes the sound diminished, sometimes it was nearer again – then all was silent. That was the worst. You could easily imagine her silent grey shadow racing along under the rising moon.

It became cold on deck.

'Look,' the Joxter said.

Somebody came careering down to the water and began darting to and fro along the bank.

'Groke's victim,' said Hodgkins. 'He'll be eaten alive.'

'Not before the eyes of a Moomin!' I cried. 'I'm going to save him!'

'No dinghy,' said Hodgkins. 'Takes too long to weigh anchor. Motor's tricky. Too late.'

But I had made my decision. I jumped on the railing and cried: 'The unknown hero doesn't ask for wreaths on his grave. But I'd appreciate a granite monument with two weeping Hemulens!' And so I dived head-first into the black water and came up under the Muddler's kettle with a clonk. With great presence of mind I hastily scooped out the Irish stew and then set my course straight as a torpedo to the shore, pushing the kettle along before me with my snout.

'Courage!' I cried. 'The Moomins are coming! There's something rotten in a country that allows its Grokes to eat the citizens!'

Pebbles and stones came rattling down the mountainside. The Groke's hunting song had ceased, and I could already hear her puffing and panting as she came galloping nearer and nearer . . .

'The kettle!' I shouted to the victim.

He took the jump, and the kettle sank to its handles.

Somebody reached for my tail in the darkness ... Ho! Glorious feat! Lonely deed! I started on the heroic journey back to *The Oshun Oxtra*, where my friends stood waiting breathless with excitement.

The rescued person was extremely heavy.

I swam with all my might, using a rotating tail stroke and rhythmic stomach movements. Like a Moomin wind I swept along, was hauled aboard, tumbled down on the deck and the kettle was emptied, while the Groke stood howling out her disappointment on the shore. (She couldn't swim.) Hodgkins lit the kerosene lamp to see whom I had rescued.

I think it was one of the worst moments of my stormy youth. Because on the wet deck before me, in a bonnet decorated with feathers and cherries, sat the Hemulen.

I had saved the life of the Hemulen.

In my first fright I raised my tail in the 45-degree angle I had been taught, but the next moment I remembered that I was a free Moomin and said nonchalantly: 'Really! Quite a surprise! I'd never have believed it!'

'Believed what?' asked the Hemulen, and shook some Irish stew out of her umbrella.

40

'That I'd rescue you. I mean, that your life was to be saved by me,' I said. 'I mean, did you get my letter?'

'I've never seen you before, young man,' said the Hemulen. 'And I haven't had any letter from you. You probably forgot to put a stamp on it. Or to write the address on the cover. Or to put it in the post box. You probably cannot write at all.'

'Do you two know each other?' Hodgkins carefully asked.

'*No*,' said the Hemulen. 'I'm the Hemulen's aunt, and I know only grown-up and sensible people. Who's been slopping jelly all over the deck? Bring me a rag, you there; I'll have to clean it up.'

Hodgkins rushed forward with the Joxter's pyjamas, and the Hemulen Aunt proceeded to scrub the deck with them.

We watched her in silence.

'Didn't I tell you of my forebodings?' the Joxter finally mumbled.

At this the Hemulen Aunt turned round and said:

'Shut up, you, please. You're much too small to smoke. You ought to drink milk, that's healthy, and it would save you from shaky paws, a yellow nose, and a bald tail. That's what smokers get. You're lucky to have me aboard. We're going to keep things in order from now on!'

'Must take a peek at the glass,' Hodgkins mumbled. He slunk unto the steering cabin and locked the door behind him.

But the glass had fallen forty notches, and it didn't dare go up again until the Niblings had left.

I'll tell you presently.

*

'Well, that's how far I've come,' said Moominpappa in his ordinary voice, and looked up from his manuscript.

'It *will* be a best-seller!' said Moomintroll, and looked proudly at his friends, Sniff and Snufkin. 'Do you think we're going to be rich?'

'Millionaires!' Moominpappa answered earnestly.

'Then we ought to share the money,' Sniff said. 'Because you've made my father, the Muddler, the hero.'

'I thought the Joxter's the hero,' Snufkin said. 'What a father! In every inch myself!'

'Your old daddies are simply so much background!' Moomintroll cried, and gave Sniff a kick under the table. 'They can be glad they're put in at all!'

'Who's put in?' Moominmamma asked at the kitchen door. 'And who's put out?'

'Daddy's reading about his life,' Moomintroll said.

'Is it fun?' asked Moominmamma.

'Terribly.'

'That's good,' said Moominmamma. 'Only don't read

anything that could set the youngsters a bad example. Just say "dash, dash, dash" instead in such places. Do you want your pipe?'

'Don't let him smoke!' shouted Sniff. 'The Hemulen Aunt says all smokers get shaky paws, yellow nose and bald tail.'

'I'm not so sure,' said Moominmamma. 'He's smoked all his life, and he's neither shaky, yellow or bald. All nice things are good for you.'

And she lit Moominpappa's pipe for him and opened the window for the evening breeze. Then she returned whistling to the kitchen to brew some coffee.

'How could you forget the Muddler at the launching!' Sniff said reproachingly. 'Did his button collection ever become sorted again?'

'Oh, many times,' answered Moominpappa. 'He was always inventing new systems. He arranged them by colour, by size, by form, by material, and by how much he liked them.'

'Great,' said Sniff.

'What worries me is that my father had his pyjamas full of jelly,' Snufkin said. 'Then what did he sleep in?'

'Mine,' said Moominpappa, and puffed out a large cloud of smoke.

Sniff yawned.

'Who'll come bat-hunting?' he asked.

'All right,' Snufkin said.

' 'Bye, Father,' said Moomintroll.

Moominpappa remained on the verandah. He sat thinking for a while, then he took out his memoir-pen and continued the story of his youth.

*

The next morning the Hemulen Aunt was devastatingly cheerful. At six o'clock we awoke to her trumpeting:

'Good morning! Good morning!! Good morning, everybody!!! And what are our plans for today? What about a little sock-darning contest on deck in the sunshine? I've looked in your sea-chests, you know. Or a nice history quiz? Good, good, good! And what's the fare today? Something healthy, I hope?'

(I think we liked her better when she was angry.)

'Coffee,' said the Muddler.

'*Porridge*,' said the Hemulen Aunt. 'Coffee's for the old and shaky.'

'I knew a chap once who died of porridge,' mumbled the Joxter. 'It stuck in his throat and choked him.'

'I wonder what your parents would say if they saw you take coffee first thing in the morning,' said the Hemulen Aunt. 'But I suppose you're badly brought up. Or not brought up at all. Or born impossible to bring up.'

'I'm born under special stars,' I said. 'I was found in a small shell padded with velvet.'

'My parents were lost in a spring-cleaning! Excuse me!' said the Muddler.

'When I last heard from my family it was at war with a park keeper,' said the Joxter.

'Hmph,' said Hodgkins. (By which I suppose he meant that parents are best discussed either when you're quite small or else old and shaky enough to be allowed coffee in the morning.)

The Hemulen Aunt looked at us over her glasses.

'From now on I'm going to take care of you,' she said.

'You needn't,' we all shouted.

But she shook her head and said cheerfully: 'It's simply

44

my Hemulic Duty. Now I'll go and prepare a little multi-plication contest for you all!'

When the Hemulen Aunt had vanished into her cabin we curled up under the sun tent on foredeck and tried to comfort each other. We left *The Oshun Oxtra* to take care of herself for a while.

'By my tail!' I said. 'I'll never save anybody in the dark again!'

'Too late now,' said the Joxter. 'One of these days she'll throw my pipe overboard and put me to work. I'm sure there are no limits to what she'll do.'

'Maybe we'll meet the Groke again?' the Muddler said hopefully. 'Or just somebody else who'll be so kind as to eat her? Excuse me! Was that rude of me?'

'H'm,' said Hodgkins.

We sat silent.

'If only I'd be a great man,' I said. 'Great and famous. Then I needn't take any notice of her.'

'How does one get famous?' the Joxter asked.

'Oh, just by doing something that nobody else has been able to do.'

'For instance?' asked the Joxter.

'Inventing a flying houseboat,' said Hodgkins with shining eyes.

'I believe it's a bore to be famous,' said the Joxter. 'Perhaps it's fun at first, but then I suppose you get used to it, and soon you're sick of it. Like on a merry-go-round.'

'What's that?' I asked.

'Don't you know?' said Hodgkins. 'Very interesting invention. I'll show you the principle of the thing.'

He produced a pencil and some paper.

(Hodgkins knew all about motors and engines! He liked them, too. I've always felt a little awed by them. A water-wheel is all right, but there I draw the line. Even a zipper is a bit suspicious. The Joxter's grandfather once had a pair of trousers with a zipper, and one day the zipper stuck, for ever.) I was about to express some such thoughts to my friends when a curious sound made us turn round.

It was a low, half-muffled howl, like somebody bellowing through a tin tube. Its tone was definitely menacing.

Hodgkins looked over the railing and uttered the single ominous word: 'Niblings!'

Here a short explanation may be necessary, even if these are well-known facts to all sensible people.

While we were having a rest in the shade under the sun tent *The Oshun Oxtra* had slowly drifted down to the river mouth where the Niblings lived. The Nibling is a social animal and detests being alone. He lives under river beds, digging tunnels with his teeth and forming rather happy colonies. He's almost as good at building things as I am. He's rather good-natured, except that he cannot keep himself from chewing and gnawing at things, particularly strange and unknown things.

And the Nibling has one bad habit: he's fond of chew-

ing off noses if they're too long (for his taste). So we felt a little nervous, for obvious reasons.

'Keep in the tin!' shouted Hodgkins to the Muddler.

The Oshun Oxtra stopped and lay quite still in a great swarm of Niblings. They looked us over in silence, treading water and fanning their whiskers.

'Please make way for us,' Hodgkins said.

But the Niblings only drew closer around the houseboat, and then a couple of them started to climb the side. They had suckers on their feet.

When the first Nibling poked its head over the railing the Hemulen Aunt appeared on deck again.

'What's all this?' she asked. 'Who're those fellows? I can't have them coming aboard to disturb our multiplication contest.'

'Don't frighten them! They'll be angry,' Hodgkins said.

'*I'm* angry,' said the Hemulen Aunt. 'Away, away! Be off with you!' And she knocked the nearest Nibling over its head with her umbrella handle.

At once all the Niblings turned to look at the Hemulen Aunt. It was obvious that they contemplated her nose. When they had contemplated it long enough they emitted once more their curious muffled tin-tube bellow. And then everything happened very quickly.

Thousands of Niblings came swarming aboard. We saw the Hemulen Aunt lose her balance, and in a few seconds, wildly waving her umbrella, she was carried away on a living carpet of hairy Nibling backs. With a loud scream she tipped over the railing and disappeared. A moment later there wasn't a single Nibling to be seen.

All was silent, and *The Oshun Oxtra* continued on its course.

'Well,' said the Joxter. 'Why didn't you rescue her?'

My chivalry prompted me to rush to her aid, but my bad and natural instincts told me it wouldn't be of any use.

'It's too late now,' I mumbled. And so it was.

'Mphm,' said Hodgkins a little uncertainly.

'And that's that,' said the Joxter.

'A sorry end,' I said.

'Excuse me, was that my fault?' asked the Muddler. 'I said, didn't I, that I hoped somebody would be so kind as to eat her?'

Well – what would you have done?

I had saved her life once, and a Groke really is something very much worse than a Nibling. Niblings aren't so bad, in fact. ... Perhaps she would enjoy the change? Perhaps she would even look nicer with a small nose?

The sun shone peacefully, and we started to scrub the deck. It was quite sticky from the Niblings' suckered feet. Then we brewed enormous quantities of good, black, strong coffee.

The Oshun Oxtra seemed to be surrounded by hundreds and hundreds of small, flat islands.

'There's no end of them,' I said. 'Where are we going?'

'Anywhere. . . . Nowhere. . . .' said the Joxter, and filled his pipe. 'What about it? We're all right, aren't we?'

Yes, of course. But still . . .

Great talent and an unquiet heart are often combined. My heart has always longed for new places and new acquaintances.

I sat in the prow looking ahead, while I pondered over my experiences so far. They were as follows:

1. Try to have your Moomin babies born at an astrologically suitable moment, and give them a romantic entry into the world.

2. People do not like to hear about Hemulens when they have other things to do.

3. You never can tell what aneroid barometers may be caught in any net.

4. Never paint a coffee tin simply because there's some paint left over.

5. All big animals are not dangerous.

6. All small animals are not afraid.

7. Try to avoid saving people in the dark.

While I sat sorting out these remarkable truths of life the houseboat rounded the last of the small islands – and suddenly my heart took a jump straight into my throat and stuck there.

Before us lay the Ocean, blue, wide and glittering!

'Hodgkins!' I shouted. 'Ocean ahead!'

'It's too big!' said the Muddler and vanished into his

tin. 'Excuse me! It tickles my eyes and I don't know what to think!'

The Joxter came on deck and wondered. He had never seen the Ocean before.

'How blue it is,' he said. 'Let's steer straight ahead and just roll and sleep and never arrive anywhere!'

'You're talking like a Hattifattener,' Hodgkins said.

'A what?' I asked.

'A Hattifattener,' answered Hodgkins. 'Never seen one? No peace, no rest. Always travelling. Travel and travel without a word. Dumb.'

'How strange,' I said. 'What a curious world it is.'

'Indeed,' said Hodgkins.

We found a harbour in a little round cove like a polished tub between the towering rocks and cliffs.

And then we went ashore to gather sea-shells. The beach was full of red and yellow sea-weed, of transparent jelly-fish and crabs and sea-urchins.

We admired the sand that was elegantly raked in little wavy stripes by the sea spooks. We climbed up and down among the cliffs that were smooth as silk and quite warm in the basking evening sun. The Muddler went wading along the beach to look for curious pebbles.

I'm sure my son Moomintroll has inherited my taste for beaches. I feel proud of him when he goes pearl-diving or cave-discovering or salvaging wreckage! But to be out at sea and to have only the horizon before one's eyes is often a little tedious to Moomins. We like changing things, all that is unexpected and strange and mixed-up, like beaches, and sunsets, and spring.

Now evening came, very slowly and carefully, to give the day ample time to go to bed. Small clouds lay strewn

over the sky like dabs of pink whipped cream. They were
reflected in the ocean that rested calm and smooth. It
looked quite harmless.

'Have you ever seen a cloud really close?' I asked.

'No,' said Hodgkins. 'Damp and chilly, I expect.'

'I think they're more like blanc-mange,' said the Joxter.

We sat talking on a rock. The air was filled with the tang of sea-weed and of something else that could only have been the ocean smell.

I felt so happy that I wasn't even afraid it wouldn't last.

'Don't you feel good?' I asked.

'Rather,' Hodgkins answered. (I knew by that that he was exceedingly and enormously happy.)

In that moment I caught sight of a whole flotilla of small ships putting out to sea. Light as butterflies they went gliding away over their own reflections. All were manned by a silent crew: little grey-white beings huddled close together and staring out towards the horizon.

'Hattifatteners,' Hodgkins said.

'Hattifatteners!' I whispered excitedly. 'Putting out on their endless voyages . . .'

'Mind you don't touch them if there's a thunderstorm about,' said Hodgkins. 'Makes them electric. Sting like nettles.'

'They used to live a wicked life,' said the Joxter.

'A wicked life?' I repeated with interest. 'How?'

'I don't quite know,' said the Joxter. 'Trampling down people's gardens and drinking beer and so on, I suppose.'

We sat there for a long time looking after the Hattifatteners sailing out towards the horizon. I really couldn't help it, but I felt a vague desire to join them on their voyage and to share their wicked life for a while. But I didn't say it.

'Well, and what about tomorrow?' asked the Joxter. 'Do we sail?'

Hodgkins looked at *The Oshun Oxtra*. 'There might be a storm,' he said a little dubiously.

'Let's toss,' said the Joxter. 'Muddler! Won't you lend us a button from your collection?'

The Muddler jumped out of the water and started to empty his pockets on the rock.

'One's enough, dear nephew,' Hodgkins said.

'Take your choice, folks,' said the Muddler happily. 'Two or four holes? Bone, plush, wood, glass, metal or mother-of-pearl? One-coloured, mottled, speckled, spotted, striped or checkered? Round, concave, convex, flat, octagonal, or . . .'

'Just a trouser button,' said the Joxter. 'Here goes. Right side upwards: we sail. What's upwards?'

'The holes,' said the Muddler, peering close at the button in the dusk.

'Yes,' I said, 'but what else?'

Just then the Muddler whisked his whiskers so that the button disappeared in a crack.

'Excuse me!' he exclaimed. 'Have another, please.'

'No, thanks,' said the Joxter. 'You can't toss more than once for anything. We'll let fate decide, because I'm sleepy.'

The night that followed aboard *The Oshun Oxtra* wasn't very pleasant.

When I went to bed I found my sheets all sticky and messy with some kind of treacly substance. The door-handles were sticky, too, and so were my slippers and my tooth-brush, and Hodgkins' log-book simply wouldn't open at all.

'Nephew,' he said. 'You haven't done these cabins very well today.'

'Excuse me!' replied the Muddler reproachingly. 'I haven't done them at all!'

'My tobacco's a single horrible, smeary mess,' exploded the Joxter, who loved to smoke a last pipe in bed.

At last we calmed down and tried to curl up in the driest places. But all night we were disturbed by strange noises and thumpings that seemed to come from the steering cabin.

I awoke to a terrible banging and clanging of the ship's bell.

'Rise up, rise up! All hands on deck!' shouted the Muddler outside my door. 'Water everywhere! So big! A lone, lone sea! And I left my best pen-wiper on the beach! My little pen-wiper's laying there all alone ...'

We rushed out.

The Oshun Oxtra lay drifting in the open sea. No land was in sight. Our anchor-rope was torn off.

'Now I'm angry,' Hodgkins said. 'Really and truly. Angrier than ever before in my life. Somebody's *bitten* off the anchor-rope.'

We looked at each other in mute reproach.

'You know my teeth aren't big enough,' I said.

'And I've got a knife, so it wouldn't have been very practical to gnaw at the rope, would it?' said the Joxter.

'It wasn't me!' cried the Muddler. We always took the Muddler at his word, because nobody had ever heard him tell a fib (not even about his collection). I expect he hadn't the imagination.

Just then we heard a little cough behind us, and when we turned round a small Nibling was sitting under the sun-tent.

'I see,' Hodgkins said grimly. 'That explains the log-book. But why the anchor-rope?'

'I'm teething,' the little Nibling answered shyly. 'I *had* to gnaw at something.'

'But why the anchor-rope?' Hodgkins repeated.

'It looked so old and worn so I thought you wouldn't mind,' said the Nibling.

'Why did you stow away when the other Niblings left?' I asked.

'I couldn't say,' answered the Nibling. 'I'm often having ideas that I can't explain.'

'And where did you hide?' the Joxter wondered.

'In your excellent binnacle,' said the Nibling. (Yes; the binnacle was quite sticky, too.)

'Nibling,' I said a little severely. 'What'll your mother say when she sees that you've run away?'

'She'll cry, I suppose,' said the Nibling.

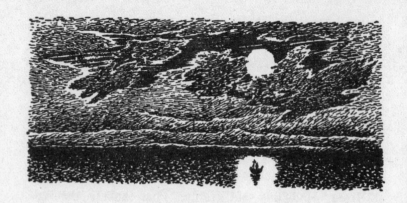

CHAPTER 4

In which the description of my Ocean voyage culminates in a magnificent tempest and ends in a terrible surprise.

STRAIGHT across the Ocean *The Oshun Oxtra* ploughed her lonely wake. One day after another went bobbing by, each one as sunny and sleepy and blue as the next. Schools of sea spooks crossed our course, and now and then a tittering trail of mermaids appeared in our wake. We fed them with oatmeal.

I liked to take my turn at the helm sometimes at nightfall. Often I could see the Joxter's pipe aglow in the dark when he came astern and sat down by my side.

'You'll have to admit that it's fun to be lazy,' he said one night, and knocked the ashes from his pipe against the railing.

'Who's lazy?' I asked. 'I'm steering. And you're smoking.'

'Wherever you're steering us,' said the Joxter.

'That's quite another matter,' I replied (I've always had

a logical mind). 'Don't say you're having Forebodings again.'

'No,' said the Joxter. 'It's all the same to me where we go. All places are all right. G'night.'

'See you tomorrow,' I said.

When Hodgkins relieved me at dawn I asked him if he didn't think it strange that the Joxter should take so little interest in things in general.

'I don't know about that,' said Hodgkins. 'Perhaps he's interested enough in everything. Only he doesn't overdo it. To *us* there's always something that is very important. When you were small you wanted to *know*. Now you want to *become*. I want to *do*. The Muddler likes his belongings. The Nibling likes other people's belongings.'

'And the Joxter likes to do forbidden things,' I reminded him.

'Yes,' said Hodgkins. 'But even they're not very important to him. He's just living.'

'Mm,' I replied.

It was the first time Hodgkins had talked about anything but practical matters. But soon he became himself again.

Later in the day the Muddler came up with the idea that we should send a wire to the Nibling's mother.

'No address. No telegraph office,' Hodgkins said.

'Oh, no, sure,' said the Muddler. 'How stupid of me! Excuse me!' And he disappeared in his tin again. Although he was a little pink we could see that he blushed.

'What's a telegraph office?' asked the Nibling, who now shared the tin with the Muddler. 'Can you eat it?'

'Don't ask me!' said the Muddler. 'It's something big and intricate. It's where you can send all kinds of little signs to other places from. . . . And then they change into words.'

'How do you send them?' asked the Nibling.

'Through the air!' said the Muddler gesticulating. 'Not a single one gets lost on the way!'

'Dear me,' said the Nibling.

After that he sat for the rest of the day craning his neck to catch sight of some telegraph signs. That was why he was the first to see the three clouds.

They came flapping towards us in a small, frightened huddle – and after them came a black cloud looking very sharp and evil.

'It's a wolf chasing three little lambs,' said the Joxter lazily.

'How terrible! Can't we save them?' cried the Muddler. (He was only a child and believed all that was said to him.)

But Hodgkins wanted to amuse his nephew. He made a running noose on a light rope, and when the first of the clouds came sailing over us he threw the rope like a lariat after it. (Which shows once again that Hodgkins wasn't always his usual self.)

We were a bit surprised when the rope caught the cloud round the middle and held it!

'Well, I say,' said Hodgkins.

'Pull!' cried the Muddler. 'Save the lamb from the wolf! Save all three of them!'

And Hodgkins pulled the cloud aboard, and then he caught the other two also.

The black wolf continued his course, so near that he brushed against the gilded knob on the boat-house.

There lay our three clouds in safety. They nearly

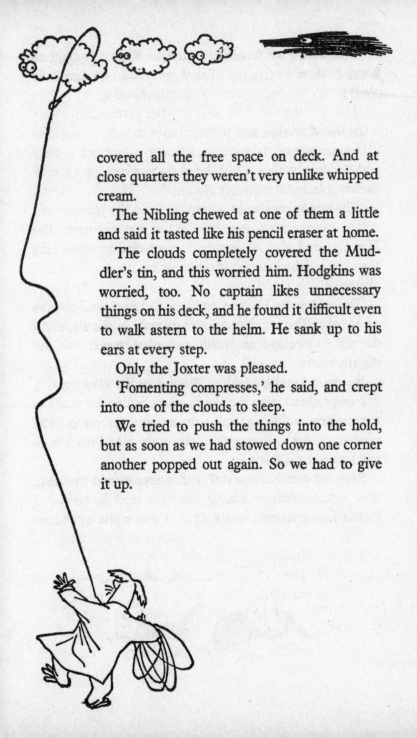

covered <u>all</u> the free space on deck. And at close quarters they weren't very unlike whipped cream.

The Nibling chewed at one of them a little and said it tasted like his pencil eraser at home.

The clouds completely covered the Muddler's tin, and this worried him. Hodgkins was worried, too. No captain likes unnecessary things on his deck, and he found it difficult even to walk astern to the helm. He sank up to his ears at every step.

Only the Joxter was pleased.

'Fomenting compresses,' he said, and crept into one of the clouds to sleep.

We tried to push the things into the hold, but as soon as we had stowed down one corner another popped out again. So we had to give it up.

(Afterwards we wondered why we hadn't thought of heaving them overboard. Thank goodness we didn't do that!)

In the afternoon, just before sunset, the sky changed to a curious yellow. It wasn't a friendly colour but a dirty and uncanny yellow. Over the horizon appeared a row of narrow, black and frowning clouds.

'The whole pack's out a-hunting,' said the Joxter.

We were sitting together under the sun-tent. The Muddler and the Nibling had succeeded in excavating their tin and had carried it astern where the deck was still cloudless.

The rolling sea had turned black and grey, and the sun grew hazy. The wind whistled anxiously in the stays. All the sea spooks and mermaids had disappeared. We felt slightly worried by it all.

'Moomin,' said Hodgkins. 'What does the glass say?'

I crept ahead over the clouds and climbed the stairs to the steering cabin. I stared at the aneroid barometer. The needle pointed at twenty-five; obviously it had tried to go still lower but had stuck.

I felt my face become stiff with suspense, and thought: 'I'm turning pale – exactly like you read in books.' I looked in the mirror. Quite right. I was white as cotton-

wool, or chalk, or newly washed Moomin feet. It was exciting.

I hurried back and said: 'Do you see that I'm deathly pale?'

'No,' said the Joxter. 'You're rather red in the face.'

'Well, what did it say?' Hodgkins asked.

'It's gone again, then,' I said a little crossly. 'Twenty-five.'

Hodgkins didn't turn pale. He said at once in a steady voice:

'Joxter! Furl the sail. Moomin! Make fast all stays, sheets, hawsers, hatches, handles, bundles and everything you can lay your hands on! The Muddler and the Nibling are to keep in their tin and put the lid on. We're in for a gale.'

'Aye, aye, sir!' we all shouted, and with a calm and manly glance at the now pale-purple sea under the yellow sky, we went to our important duties.

The gale was over us in an instant, so suddenly that *The Oshun Oxtra* dived on her nose and nearly stood on her head for a while.

I hadn't had time to take down the sun-tent, and it was torn away like a leaf and flapped out to sea. (It was a nice sun-tent. I hope somebody found it and enjoyed it.)

'Start the engine!' Hodgkins shouted through the gale. But the hatch was deep under the clouds, and I suppose the cogwheels wouldn't have fitted in anyway just then. The engine had been freakish lately.

The Muddler's tin had jammed and stuck under the railing, and every time *The Oshun Oxtra* took a dive or was lifted high on a wave-crest all his buttons, suspenders, tin-openers, and glass pearls made a terrible clatter inside. The Muddler cried that he was feeling sick, but there wasn't anything we could do about it. We could only cling to the holds we had and stare out over the darkening ocean.

The sun was gone. The horizon was gone. We were in the midst of a black and frightening turmoil with flecks of white foam flying past us everywhere like hissing ghosts.

Hodgkins clung steadily to the helm, and the Joxter and I clung to each other. The Joxter tried to shout something, but I could hear nothing but the roar of the wind. He pointed ahead.

I looked and saw a large, inflated balloon carrying us forwards with great speed. But it wasn't our sail – it was one of our clouds.

'That's the end of it,' I thought dizzily.

Then the second cloud moved. It flattened out, and in a second the gale had blown into it and stretched it to a big sail.

But it didn't burst. It stretched like another rubber balloon, and *The Oshun Oxtra* plunged forward shaking and creaking in every seam. Now we were rushing along as fast as the gale itself.

Then the third cloud took to the air, and it lifted the houseboat almost clear of the water. Like an albatross, like the Flying Dutchman, like a Moomin ghost ship we sailed on.

It all resembled a dream or a huge merry-go-round. My fright passed, and I intoned a song of victory about invincible Moomins.

When the darkness finally began to change to a morning grey I was aware that I was cold and that the Joxter had grabbed my tail in a smarting grip.

The wild roar of the hurricane had toned down to an even whistling, and the movements of *The Oshun Oxtra* told me that she was in the water once more. Two of the clouds had furled themselves again, and I could hear the buttons rattling about inside the Muddler's tin.

Another day was dawning.

I carefully moved one leg and then the other one. Both were safe and sound. Then I politely asked the Joxter to let go of my tail.

'Oh, was it yours,' he said. 'I thought it was the backstay all the time.'

A pale light was spreading over the sea and exposed the sad state of *The Oshun Oxtra*. The mast was broken. The paddles gone. My beautiful house was badly demolished, most of all the fretwork on the verandah. Worst of all, the gilt knob had disappeared from the roof top.

Torn stays swayed sadly in the wind, and the railings were smashed in several places. But between them our three clouds rested, white and round, exactly as before.

'Dear crew,' said Hodgkins solemnly. 'We have ridden out the hurricane. Let my nephew out, please!'

We took off the lid and the Muddler appeared, pitifully green in the face.

'Button of all buttons,' he said wearily. 'What have I done to be so sick? Oh, what life, what troubles, what worries! *Look* at my collection!'

The Nibling came out also, sniffed against the wind and snorted. Then he said: 'I'm hungry!'

'Excuse me!' exclaimed the Muddler. 'Just to *think* of food makes me . . .'

'Quite, quite,' said Hodgkins kindly. 'Perhaps Moomin will go and warm the pea-soup. I'll have to think. . . . *The Oshun Oxtra* nearly flew tonight. I've an idea. You know. The flying houseboat . . .'

And Hodgkins became absorbed in calculations. I made my way carefully over the deck.

It was covered with sea-weed, Nibling smear, oysters, and a few faint sea spooks. And in that moment the sun rose.

Oh, delight! I stopped outside the galley door and gave the warmth time to surge through me. I remembered the sunshine on my first day of freedom after the night of my escape. I loved the sun!

I forgot all about the pea-soup and closed my eyes where I stood. The lovely feeling penetrated out to the tip of my tail, and I thought it was worth a hurricane to have the sunshine afterwards.

But when I opened my eyes again I discovered something on starboard. Land!

Land ahead also! Soft contours of strange mountains! I stood on my head for joy and shouted:

'We're there! Land! Hodgkins!'

Suddenly we all became busy.

The Muddler's sickness ceased at once, and he began putting his tin in order. The Joxter repaired the auxiliary engine. The Nibling chewed at his own tail out of pure nervousness, and Hodgkins put me to polishing all the brass-work.

The foreign shore came nearer. There seemed to be a high mountain on it with a tower on top.

'What on earth's that?' asked the Joxter.

'Look, it's moving,' I said.

But we were too busy to worry about it.

Only when *The Oshun Oxtra* glided into harbour we gathered at the railing, after having combed our hair and brushed our teeth and tails.

And then we heard a thundering voice high above our heads:

'Ha!' it roared. 'The Groke take me if this isn't Hodgkins and his dash-dashed crew! Now I've got you!'

It was Edward the Booble. You can't imagine how angry he was.

*

'That's how life was when I was young!' said Moominpappa and closed his book.

'Read more, please!' Moomintroll cried. 'What happened then? What did the Booble do to you?'

'Next time, my boy,' Moominpappa said with an air of mystery. 'That was thrilling, eh? But you see, it's a trick all good authors use, to close a chapter at the ghastliest moment.'

This time Moominpappa had seated himself on the sandy beach with his son, Snufkin, and Sniff at his feet.

While he read to them about the terrible gale they gazed out over the sea and imagined *The Oshun Oxtra* careering along like a ghost ship, manned by their brave fathers, through the pale purple foam of the hurricane.

'How sick he must have been in his tin,' mumbled Sniff.

'It's cold here,' said Moominpappa. 'Shall we take a walk?'

They wandered off over the dry sea-weed to the point.

'Can you imitate a Nibling?' asked Snufkin.

Moominpappa tried. 'No-o,' he said. 'It didn't come right. It should sound as if from a tin tube.'

'It wasn't so far off,' said Moomintroll. 'Father, didn't you go away with the Hattifatteners later on?'

'Well,' answered Moominpappa embarrassedly, 'perhaps I did. But that was very much later. I suppose it won't come into the book at all.'

'Why not?' cried Sniff. 'Did you lead a wicked life with them?'

'Shut up,' said Moomintroll.

'Dash, dash, dash,' said Moominpappa. 'But it wasn't too wicked. Look, there's something floating in the water. Run along and see what it is!'

They ran.

'What can it be?' asked Snufkin.

66

It was a heavy and onion-shaped thing. It seemed to have floated around for a very long time, because it was covered with weeds and clams. The wood was cracked, and in a few places there were remains of gold paint. Moominpappa lifted the wooden onion in both paws and examined it carefully. His eyes grew larger and larger, and finally he covered them with one paw and sighed.

'Children,' he said solemnly and a little shakily, 'what you behold here is the knob from the roof of the boathouse of *The Oshun Oxtra*!'

'Oh,' said Moomintroll with great veneration.

'And now,' continued Moominpappa, overcome by his memories, 'now I'm going to start on a new chapter and contemplate this unique discovery in solitude. Run along and play in the cave!'

Moominpappa walked on with a springy step. He carried the knob under one arm and his Memoirs under the other.

'I've really been a strapping Moomin in my day!' he said to himself.

'And still going strong,' he added, and stamped his feet with a happy smile.

CHAPTER 5

In which (besides giving a little specimen of my intellectual powers), I describe the Mymble family and the Surprise Party which brought me some bewitching tokens of honour from the hand of the Autocrat.

PERHAPS you've noticed the peculiar way my mind works? There's simply a sudden click! – and the situation is saved. Like this one, for instance.

Here's the Booble, grumbling, bumbling and shouting at us, and here are we, looking rather foolish, and then I say (quite calmly): 'Hullo, uncle! Glad to see you again!' And of course this doesn't stop him shouting, but I don't mind at all. I just ask him whether his feet are sore still.

'You have the nerve to ask me that!' roars Edward the Booble. 'You water-flea! You nightmare! *Yes*, my feet are sore! *Yes*, my behind is sore too!'

'Well, in that case,' I answer in a perfectly controlled voice, 'in that case the present we've brought you will suit you all the better. Three genuine eider-down Booble sleeping-bags!'

(Rather smart, wasn't it?)

'Sleeping-bags? Eider-down?' Edward the Booble said suspiciously and carefully felt our clouds with one foot. 'You're deceiving me again, aren't you, you dish-rags? I suppose they're stuffed with rocks . . .'

He hauled the clouds up on the wharf and sniffed at them.

'Sit down, Edward, please!' cried Hodgkins. 'Nice and soft!'

'I've heard that before,' grumbled the Booble. 'Nice, smooth sand bottom, you said. And what was it? The hardest, knobbliest, stoniest, pestilentiallest . . .'

And Edward the Booble carefully sank down on the clouds.

'Well?' we cried expectantly.

'Hrrumph,' said the Booble sourly. 'There seem indeed to be a few soft spots. I'll sit here and think for a while until I've decided what to do with you.'

But we didn't care to wait. With great speed we made fast the hawser and stole past behind the Booble. And then we ran.

'You did rather well,' said the Joxter.

'Just an idea,' I said modestly.

'I know,' said Hodgkins. 'Empty place, this.'

Round green hills rose everywhere around us, with single big trees laden with bunches of green and yellow berries. We could see a few small straw huts huddling in the valleys between low stone walls stretching over the hillsides.

But all was silent. Not a trace of the excited crowd we had imagined would come running to look at *The Oshun Oxtra* and ourselves, and to ask us all about the hurricane.

'Perhaps Edward the Booble has frightened them away,' I said a little disappointedly.

We went up the nearest hill.

'There's a house,' said the Joxter. 'I'd like to see if the door's locked.'

It was a small hut, not very well built of board ends and large stiff leaves.

We knocked four times, but nobody opened.

'Ahoy!' Hodgkins shouted. 'Anybody home?'

Then we heard a small voice that answered: 'No, no! Nobody at all!'

'That's funny,' I said. 'Then who's talking?'

'I'm the Mymble's little daughter,' said the voice. 'But you'll have to go away quickly, because I'm not allowed to open the door to anybody until mother comes back.'

'Where's mother, then?' Hodgkins asked.

'She's gone to the garden party,' the little voice answered sadly.

'Well, why didn't she take you along?' the Muddler asked in a shocked voice. 'Are you too small?'

Then the Mymble's daughter started to cry and said: 'I've a sore throat today! Mother thought it might be diphtheria!'

'Open the door, won't you?' Hodgkins said kindly. 'We'll have a look at your throat. Don't be afraid.'

The Mymble's daughter opened the door. She had a thick woollen scarf around her neck, and her eyes were quite red.

'Let's see now,' Hodgkins said. 'Open your mouth, please. Wider, please. Say a-a-a-ah!!'

'Or typhoid fever, or cholera mother thought,' said the Mymble's daughter sadly. 'A-a-a-ah!'

'Not a spot,' Hodgkins said. 'Not even swollen. Does it hurt?'

'Terribly,' mumbled the Mymble's daughter. 'I think my throat's growing together, so I'll not be able to breathe at all, and not to eat or talk either.'

'You'll have to go to bed at once,' Hodgkins said. 'We'll find your mother for you. Immediately!'

'No, no, please don't,' the daughter cried. 'It was just a fib. I'm not ill at all. Mother left me at home because I've been a bad girl.'

'A fib? Whatever for?' Hodgkins asked in astonishment.

'To have a little fun!' said the Mymble's daughter and

started to cry once more. 'I've nothing on earth to do!'

'Can't we take her with us to that garden party?' the Joxter proposed.

'Perhaps the Mymble wouldn't like it,' I said.

'Of course she would,' said her daughter happily. 'She'll be terribly glad, because I'm sure she's forgotten it all by now.'

'Can you show us the way? To the party?' asked Hodgkins.

' 'Course I can!' said the Mymble's daughter and took off her woolly scarf. 'But we'll have to hurry, or else the King will be disappointed. The surprises must have started long ago.'

'Is he a real King?' I asked respectfully as we went at a jog trot over the hills.

'A real King?' exclaimed the Mymble's daughter. 'He's a true Autocrat and the greatest King alive. But we're allowed to call him Daddy Jones to feel more at home with him.'

'I'm going to call him Your Autocratical Majesty,' I said very earnestly. 'Imagine, to shake hands with a real King! It's the reward for my old and sincere royalist views!'

'Why do you have all these stone walls?' asked the Joxter. 'Do you want to shut people in or out?'

'No,' answered the Mymble's daughter. 'We don't use them for anything special. It's just that we like building them. My mother's brother has built nineteen miles of them. And d'you know what else he does? He's studying all letters and words from all sides. He likes to walk around them until he's quite sure of them. It takes him hours and hours to do the longest words!'

'Like otolaryngologist,' said the Joxter.

'Or kalospinterochcromatokrene,' I said.

'Oh,' said the Mymble's daughter. 'If they're *that* long he has to camp beside them for the night. He used to sleep on the ground in nothing but his long red beard. Half the beard's his cover and the other half's his mattress. In the daytime he keeps two small white mice in it, and they're so sweet that they don't have to pay any rent.'

'Most curious,' said Hodgkins. 'Have you any brothers or sisters?'

'Lots and lots,' said the Mymble's daughter. 'Nobody's been able to count them, they run so fast. Look, here we are. Promise me to tell mother that you made me come here to show you the way!'

'Certainly,' Hodgkins promised. 'What does she look like?'

'She's round,' said her daughter. 'Everything's round about her.'

We were standing before a gate, garlanded with flowers, in an exceptionally high stone wall. The gate bore a large placard reading:

DADDY JONES'S GARDEN PARTY
FREE FOR ALL!

Come in, come in, please!

THE SURPRISE PARTY OF THE YEAR –
VERY SPECIAL!

(because of the 100th Anniversary of Our Birth)

DON'T BE AFRAID
If Anything Happens ! ! !

73

'What happens?' asked the Nibling.

'Anything,' said the Mymble's daughter. 'That's the fun of it. You'll see!'

We went into the garden and looked around us.

It was wild and overgrown.

'Excuse me, are there any wild beasts?' the Muddler asked nervously.

'Much worse,' grinned the Mymble's daughter. 'I'll run along now. See you later.'

We followed carefully. A long tunnel filled with green and mysterious light led us through the thickets and bushes.

'Stop, everybody! Stay where you are!' cried Hodgkins suddenly and halted in his tracks.

An abyss yawned before us. And down there crouched a hairy and goggling Thing – on long, quivering legs – a giant spider!

'Hush! Let's see if he's angry,' whispered the Joxter and began throwing pebbles at the monster.

The spider wobbled his legs, swayed horribly and threw his eyes about (they were on stalks).

'Unnatural,' Hodgkins remarked. 'His legs. Wire springs.'

He was right. The whole spider was made of wire springs.

'Excuse me, that was almost impudent,' said the Muddler. 'As if one weren't afraid enough of *really* dangerous things!'

'One of the party surprises, I expect,' said Hodgkins and led us on with redoubled care.

At the next turn of the path hung a placard reading:

SCARED – WEREN'T YOU?

'I'd never thought a King would descend to such jokes,' I said. 'Even if he's a hundred years old. Don't let yourself be scared next time we see anything remarkable.'

'Here's a lake,' Hodgkins said. 'Artificial too.'

We looked at it with suspicion. Small brightly painted dinghies bearing the Autocratical colours lay on the beach. Friendly-looking trees were leaning out over the clear water.

'I don't quite believe it,' muttered the Joxter and chose himself an orange-coloured boat with an azure railing.

We were out in the middle of the lake when the next surprise overtook us.

A strong jet of water shot up between our boats and drenched us to the skin. The Nibling howled frightfully.

Before we reached the other beach we had four more showers, and on the shore we found another placard asking us:

WET – AREN'T YOU?

'Funny kind of garden party,' muttered Hodgkins.

'I like it,' said the Joxter. 'Daddy Jones must be a singular person.'

Now we came to a whole network of canals with a maze of bridges. In the difficult places you had to cross on rotten

old tree-trunks or on suspended lianas. But nothing special happened, except that the Nibling dived head first into a mud bank.

Suddenly the Joxter exclaimed: 'At last! Here's a new joke! But this time he won't pull *my* leg!' And the Joxter walked straight up to a big stuffed bull and gave it a smack on the muzzle.

Only the big bull wasn't stuffed. It was very much alive and gave a terrific bellow. We fled head over heels behind a dense hedge where another placard was awaiting us:

DIDN'T THINK SO – DID YOU?

By and by we became accustomed to the surprises. We wandered further and further, deeper and deeper into Daddy Jones's garden, through leafy caverns and secret hiding-places, under waterfalls and over new abysses with Bengal lights. But the Autocrat had provided his guests with other things than trap-doors, explosions, and wire spring monsters. If you looked carefully at the roots of bushes, in hollow trees and cracks in the rocks you sometimes found small nests containing one or more brightly painted or golden eggs. Each egg had a number on it.

I found numbers 67, 14, 890, 223, and 27.

It was Daddy Jones's Royal Lottery.

We all became quite crazy with egg-hunting. The Nibling found most of the eggs, but it was hard to make him understand that it would be better to save them for the draw than to eat them on the spot.

Hodgkins came a good second, then I, and then the Joxter who was too lazy to search in earnest, and lastly the Muddler whose only method consisted in hopping around.

Finally we found one end of a long red and yellow rope that was slung between the trees and tied in beautiful bows. As we followed it we began to hear a medley of happy whoops, shots, and music. The party seemed to be in full swing.

'I think I'll stay here and wait for you,' said the Nibling a little nervously. 'There's such a lot of people.'

'As you like,' said Hodgkins. 'Only keep still so we can find you again.'

We were standing at the outskirts of a great open meadow. We looked, simply enraptured. In the middle of the meadow stood a large circular house that seemed to whirl round and round. It was full of fluttering pennants and white horses in shining silver harness, and an orchestra played all the time.

'What on earth's that?' I asked excitedly.

'A merry-go-round,' Hodgkins replied. 'Don't you remember? I drew it for you once. Cross section of the engine.'

'You didn't draw it like this,' I protested. 'It's all horses and music and flags and gold!'

'*And* cog wheels,' said Hodgkins.

'Ginger ale, please?' asked a big Hemulen in a definitely unbecoming pinafore (I've always said so: Hemulens have no taste). She gave us each a glass and said importantly:

'You'll have to go and wish Daddy Jones many happy returns of the day. It's his hundredth birthday, you know.'

I took my glass of ginger ale in a shaky paw and looked up towards the Autocrat's throne. For the first time in my life I beheld a real King! He was terribly old and wrinkly and merry and he was stamping time to the music so that his throne wobbled. Under it he kept a fog horn and gave

78

a short blast every time he wished to acknowledge a toast from any one of his subjects.

We bowed to the earth, and when the fog horn ceased Hodgkins said: 'Many happy returns of the century!'

'And thank you for the greatly successful surprises, Your Autocratical Majesty,' I added in an unnatural voice and saluted with my tail.

'Cheerio!' said Daddy Jones and chuckled happily. 'Did it come off? Were you wet? What did the bull do? Did anybody fall in the treacle trap? Really, sometimes it's great fun to be King!'

'If Your Majesty allows me . . .' I started to say.

'Call Us Jones, please,' said the Autocrat. 'Hullo, my people good and true! (Blast you, stop that merry-go-round!) Come hither, all! It's time to draw the lottery prizes!'

The merry-go-round and the swings stopped, and everybody came running with their eggs.

'701!' shouted Daddy Jones. 'Who's got number 701?'

'I have,' said Hodgkins.

'Here you are, please,' said the King and handed him an excellent fret-saw of the kind he had always wanted.

I squeezed my eggs in excitement. Every time a new number was called I felt a catch in my throat – but every time it was somebody else's number. Every little black-beetle seemed to have won something or other, but not I.

The Joxter and the Muddler already had a row of prizes in front of them and were busy, because the prizes were mostly chocolate balls, marchpane Hemulens, or spun-sugar roses. And Hodgkins sat in the grass holding a heap of practical and uninteresting things in his lap.

Finally Daddy Jones rose and made a little speech:

'My dear people! Dear muddle-headed, fuzzy, and thoughtless subjects! Each of you has won exactly the things that suit him best and that he's earned. In Our centennial wisdom We have hidden the eggs in three kinds of places. Firstly, in the grass where you might stumble on them simply running about or when you are too lazy to look carefully. All those prizes are eatable. Secondly, We have hidden some eggs where they can be found with meticulous and methodical search. Those prizes are useful. And thirdly, We have chosen hiding-places that need a certain amount of imagination to find. And those prizes are of no use whatever. Now, my pig-headed, dear and silly subjects! Who of you have looked in fancy places: in the brooks, in the tree-tops, in the flower-buds, in his own pockets, or in the anthills? Who has found Numbers 67, 14, 890, 999, 223, and 27?'

'I have,' I shouted quite loudly, which made me a little embarrassed for a moment.

And shortly afterwards a smaller voice beside me said: '999!'

'Come hither, poor little Moomin,' said Daddy Jones.

'Behold the utterly useless rewards of the fantastic. Do you like them?'

'Terribly, Your Majesty,' I breathed.

My prizes were enchanting. I think number 27 was the nicest. It was a drawing-room decoration: a small meerschaum tram on a coral pedestal. You could keep safety pins on the front platform. Number 67 was a champagne whisk beset with garnets. The other prizes were a shark's tooth, a preserved smoke ring, and an organ-grinding handle inlaid with mother-of-pearl. Can you understand my bliss?

'And what about me?' asked the Mymble's daughter who had Number 999.

'Little girl,' said Daddy Jones gravely. 'You have drawn the capital prize. You are entitled to kiss Daddy Jones on the nose.'

The Mymble's daughter shyly climbed on the Autocrat's lap and kissed him on his old autocrat nose. The multitude cheered madly and started eating their prizes.

It was a really lavish, grand and sumptuous garden party. At dusk, coloured lanterns were lighted all over the Garden of Surprises, and everybody played or danced or sang and forgot all about morning.

I was milling around with the others when I perceived a female person who seemed wholly built of round pieces. I went up to her, bowed and asked:

'Excuse me, Madam, do you happen to be the Mymble?'

'Herself!' said the Mymble laughing. 'Tumble and bumble, what a lot I've eaten! Listen, Moomin, weren't you sorry to get such peculiar prizes?'

'I like them,' I replied. 'And think of the honour! Not to mention your daughter who won the main prize.'

'She's a credit to the family,' said the Mymble proudly.

'So you're not angry with her any more?' I asked.

'Angry?' said the Mymble surprised. 'I'm never angry with anybody, at least not for long. I simply haven't the time! Eighteen, nineteen kiddies to wash, put to bed, button up and button down, feed, wipe the nose of, and the Groke knows what. No, my young Moomin, I'm enjoying myself all the time!'

'And what a singular brother you have,' I continued by way of conversation.

'Brother?' said the Mymble.

'Yes, your daughter's maternal uncle,' I explained.

'Who camps beside all the longest words until he's studied them enough, and who sleeps in his long red beard where two white mice lodge free of rent.'

The Mymble started to laugh heartily and said: 'What a daughter I have, indeed! She's been pulling your leg, Moomin! She hasn't any uncle that I know of. Cheerio, I'll have to try the merry-go-round!'

And the Mymble collected as many of her children that her broad lap could hold and mounted one of the red carriages drawn by a dapple grey horse.

'What a remarkable lady,' said the Joxter with sincere admiration.

On the horse sat the Muddler looking quaint.

'Well?' I asked. 'Isn't it fun?'

'Yes thanks, grand,' said the Muddler. 'I'm certainly having a swell time. But this going round and round makes you a bit sick in the end. . . . It's a pity!'

'How many rounds have you been on?' I asked.

'Don't know,' replied the Muddler exhaustedly. 'A lot! Such a lot! Oh, here I go again!'

'Time to go home,' said Hodgkins. 'Where's the King?'

But Daddy Jones was busy at the swings, so we left discreetly.

(Except for the Joxter who wasn't able to tear himself from the company of the merry and laughing Mymble.)

In the park we found our Nibling. He had dug himself a hole in the ground and gone to sleep.

'Hullo!' I said. 'You haven't taken out your prizes.'

'Prizes?' said the Nibling and blinked his eyes.

'Your eggs,' said Hodgkins. 'You had a dozen.'

'I ate them,' answered the Nibling shyly. 'I hadn't anything else to do while I waited for you.'

I've often wondered since what the Nibling's prizes would have been and who got them when he didn't ask for them.

Perhaps Daddy Jones saved them for his next centennial garden party.

CHAPTER 6

In which I become a Royal Outlaw Colonist and show remarkable presence of mind when meeting the Ghost of Horror Island.

AT dawn the following day a uniformed Hemulen of the Autocrat Guards knocked on the door of our cabin and shouted: 'Telegram! Express telegram for Mr Hodgkins!'

Hodgkins calmly put on his captain's cap and opened the message. It read:

OUR ATTENTION DIRECTED FACT HODGKINS FIRST-CLASS INVENTOR PLEASE PLACE TALENTS IMMEDIATELY AUTOCRAT JONESS SERVICE URGENT

'Excuse me,' said the Muddler, 'but he doesn't seem to be any grand letter-writer. There's a lot of small words and stops missing.'

'That's how express telegrams are,' explained Hodgkins.

85

'No time to put in all the words. It's a very good telegram.'

'But you said yourself that not a single letter's lost on the way,' said the Nibling.

'Too long to explain now,' said Hodgkins. 'I'll have to see the King.'

'May I put in the small words in your express telegram while you're away?' asked the Muddler.

'Please do,' said Hodgkins. 'But carefully.'

'Are you going to stay with the King?' I asked anxiously.

'Don't know yet,' Hodgkins said abstractedly, polishing his zipper. 'Depends. New tools ... tons of nuts and bolts ... miles of wire spring ... Might improve the house-boat ...'

'And what about me?' I said.

'You?' said Hodgkins surprised. 'You'll stay too, of course. As Royal Moominhouse constructor. We'll found a colony. We'll be colonists.'

'M-m,' I replied and went ashore to visit the Mymble. I kicked a stone before me all the way and pretended it was a king, until I suddenly remembered that I was a royalist. God save the King, I said quickly three times to myself. The stone's a colonist, the Groke take him.

'Morning,' said the Mymble's daughter. She was standing at the pump washing her small brothers and sisters. 'Have you swallowed a lemon?'

'We're not explorers any more, we're colonists,' I said.

'Pestilence,' said the Mymble's daughter. 'That's bad. What do colonists do?'

'I don't know,' I said. 'Probably something silly. I think it would be better to follow the Hattifatteners, lone as the desert wind or the mountain eagle.'

'I'm coming with you!' said the Mymble's daughter.

'There's a lot of difference between Hodgkins and you,' I said (markedly).

'Yes, isn't there,' cried the Mymble's daughter happily. 'Mother! Where are you?'

'Here,' said the Mymble and put her head out from under a large leaf. 'How many have you washed?'

'Half,' said her daughter. 'I'll leave it at that. Because this Moomin has asked me to go round the world with him.'

'Well, as a matter of fact . . .' I managed to say.

But the Mymble said wonderingly: 'You don't say! Then you won't be back for dinner?'

'Oh no, mother,' said the Mymble's daughter. 'Next time we meet I'll be grown-up and the biggest Mymble in the world! When do we start?'

'I suppose colony life isn't so bad after all,' I said faintly. 'We're a Mymble short. So if you'd rather like to become just a colonist . . .'

She rather liked it.
Mymbles like anything.

About two nautical miles north of Daddy Jones's kingdom there lies a moderately big, heart-shaped island. We colonized it.

We moored ship in the cove (the map will show you), and Hodgkins remained aboard and started inventing trap doors for the Autocrat. The Joxter settled down in an apple tree on the eastern side, and I moved the Moominhouse from the boat to the western shore. The Muddler's tin was rolled up on the hill in the middle of the island, because he was a little scared to live near the edges, he said. The rest of the island belonged to the Mymble's daughter – except the tip of the heart which we chose for a secret meeting-place.

We held the first council (to make laws for the colony) on a Thursday at dusk. Each of us had a large sea-shell to sit on, and Hodgkins pulled the bung from a hollow tree that we had filled with a supply of Daddy Jones's home-made palm wine.

The Muddler served us corn cobs (my favourite food) and plum cake. A bright orange moon was poking its head over the horizon. The night was quite warm.

'And now, what is a colonist, please?' I asked.

'Colonists are strangers in a country that do not quite like to live alone,' explained the Joxter. 'So they move together in the wilderness and start quarrelling, I believe. I suppose they like that better than not to have anybody to quarrel with.'

'Do we have to quarrel?' asked the Muddler. 'I wouldn't like it. Excuse me! It's so sad!'

'Bless me, no,' said Hodgkins. 'We're going to live in peace.'

"Exactly,' said the Joxter. 'And sometimes we'll make something unusual and sudden happen. Then peace again. What?'

'Exactly!' we all said.

'My tree on the sunside,' the Joxter continued dreamily. 'Songs and apples and sleeping late, you know. Nobody buzzing around and telling me that things cannot be postponed. . . . I'm going to let things run themselves.'

'And do they?' asked the Muddler.

'*Do* they?' exclaimed the Joxter. 'Just leave them alone and you'll be surprised. The oranges grow, and the flowers open, and now and then a new Joxter is born to eat them and smell them. And the sun shines on it all.'

'Great big oranges,' said the Nibling. (He sat by himself drinking milk, because he was too small for palm wine.)

'You, little Nibling,' said Hodgkins kindly. 'You're going home to your mother. Tomorrow morning on the packet boat.'

'You don't say,' said the Nibling and sipped his milk.

'But I'll stay,' said the Mymble's daughter. 'Until I'm grown-up. Hodgkins, can't you invent anything to make Mymbles grow terribly big?'

'A small one's enough,' I said.

'That's what mother says, too,' she replied. 'D'you know, I was born in a clam and wasn't bigger than a waterflea when mother found me in her aquarium!'

'Fibbing again,' I said. 'I know perfectly well that people grow inside their mothers, like apple seeds.'

'Any way you like,' said the Mymble's daughter.

Just then the Joxter half-rose and said:

'Wait a bit! Here's something funny . . .'

A ragged cloud passed across the moon. We listened intently. Everything was silent.

'You're trying to scare us!' said the Muddler. 'We're the only colonists on this island.'

'Perhaps,' said the Joxter and sat down again. 'I just had a kind of feeling that somebody went sneaking over the sand. Like apple seeds, did you say?'

'Yes, or a plum-stone,' I replied. 'Are you sure you're mistaken? Didn't you see anybody?'

'Something grey and misty, perhaps – I don't really know,' mumbled the Joxter. 'It glided, sort of.'

'I'm cold,' said the Muddler nervously. 'Excuse me, won't anybody take me home?'

'You can stay with me tonight,' said the Mymble's daughter. 'I'm terribly brave.'

'Is your house strong?' asked the Muddler.

'Concrete and stone!' she answered.

(Of course we all knew that she was lodging under a big leaf.)

But the Muddler felt easier, and they walked off together with the Nibling, as soon as we had tied an address label to his tail for the voyage and kissed him on the nose. (It was greatly to his honour that he didn't bite anybody's snout for a farewell.)

'Best regards to your mother,' Hodgkins said. 'And don't sink the packet boat.'

'I shan't,' said the Nibling happily, and so he went.

'Well,' Hodgkins said and drained his wine cup. 'I suppose we'll call it a day, too. The laws can wait.'

'Couldn't we have an outlaw colony?' asked the Joxter. 'Laws are always a bother.'

'Ought to break them first, of course,' Hodgkins said. 'I mean, something has to go wrong before you know a law is called for.'

'But if you do something the wrong way and nothing goes wrong afterwards?' I asked. 'It happens, you know. Does that call for a law, too?'

'A poser, that,' Hodgkins said. 'Good night, everybody!'

We separated at the Muddler's tin, that stood empty and abandoned on the hill-top (as usual he had forgotten to put the lid on).

I walked on alone to my house.

It stood beautifully outlined against the sky between the cliff-tops by the beach. The sand glittered in the moonlight, and all the shadows were pitch-black. I mounted the stairs to the former steering-cabin and opened the window. The night was so silent that you could hear the big furry moths brushing their wings.

Then the door downstairs gave a creak.

A cold draught swept up from below and breathed down my neck.

Now, afterwards, I'm sure I wasn't scared; I simply took natural precautions. Determinedly I crawled under the bed and waited.

Soon the stairs began to creak also. One small creak, and then another. There were nineteen steps, I knew, because the staircase had been quite a complicated affair to build (it was a winding staircase, of course). I counted nineteen creaks, then everything was silent once more, and I thought: 'It's standing by the door.'

*

Here Moominpappa stopped reading. The thrill was intense.

'Sniff,' he said, 'turn up the wick, please. Do you know, my paws become all wet when I read about that ghastly experience!'

'Then it was a ghost?' asked Moomintroll who had pulled his quilt up to his ears.

'It was a ghost,' replied Moominpappa seriously.

'Did my daddy the Joxter like that Mymble very much?' Snufkin suddenly asked.

'I think he did,' said Moominpappa a little thoughtfully.

'More than me?' asked Snufkin.

'He never saw you, you know,' said Moominpappa. 'I mean – if he'd seen you I suppose he'd liked you more still. But Snufkin dear, don't look so downcast. Wait a bit, I'll show you something!'

Moominpappa went to the big corner cabinet and

started a search on the lowest shelf. After a while he returned and laid a glistening white shark's tooth on Snufkin's bed.

'It's yours,' he said. 'Your daddy used to admire it.'

'What a good taste he had. Thanks a lot!' Snufkin said. He was happy again.

'What became of the other lottery prizes?' asked Sniff. 'The meerschaum tram's under the drawing-room pier-glass, but what about the others?'

'Well, we never had any champagne,' Moominpappa thoughtfully replied. 'So I expect the whisk is still some-where at the back of the kitchen drawer. And the smoke-ring evaporated in a few years . . .'

'But the organ-grinding handle!' cried Sniff.

Moominpappa looked at him.

'If I only knew your birthday,' he said. 'Your daddy the Muddler always was a careless one with calendars.'

'I can choose any day,' Sniff said.

'All right, you may expect a mysterious parcel any day,' Moominpappa said. 'Shall I read some more?'

Moomintroll nodded.

And Moominpappa started to read again.

*

The door opened slightly and very slowly, and a little grey wisp of smoke floated through the crack and curled up on my carpet. Two pale and shining eyes blinked at the top of the curl. I saw it all very clearly from my hiding-place under the bed.

'It's a ghost,' I said to myself. And funnily enough it was much less frightening to look at him than it had been to listen to him coming up the stairs.

The room had suddenly grown cold with an icy draught, and the ghost sneezed.

I don't know how you'd have felt, but for my part I immediately lost much of my respect. So I crawled out from under the bed and said: 'Cold night, sir!'

'Yes,' replied the ghost in an annoyed tone. 'A bleak night of fate resounding with the horrible wails of the phantoms of the gorge!'

'What can I do for you?' I asked politely.

'On a night of fate like this,' the ghost continued stubbornly, 'the forgotten bones are rattling on the silent beach!'

'Whose bones?' I asked (still very politely).

'The *forgotten* bones,' said the ghost. 'Pale horror grins over the damned island! Mortal, beware!' The ghost uncurled, gave me a terrible look and floated back towards the half-open door. The back of his head met the door-jamb with a resounding bang.

'Oop!' said the ghost.

I didn't hide my delight.

With a last hiss the ghost glided downstairs and out into the moonlight. Down on the ground he turned and bade me farewell with three horrible laughs.

'I'll have to tell the others tomorrow,' I said to myself. 'Perhaps Hodgkins can invent a ghost-proof lock to put on my door.'

Hodgkins took the matter more seriously than I had expected. 'That kind of a ghost can be troublesome enough,' he said. 'If you laugh at him. When he would like to frighten you.'

'Do you know what he's done tonight?' asked the Joxter. 'He's painted a skull and crossbones and the word "poison" on the Muddler's tin, and the Muddler's feeling very offended and says he isn't that kind of person.'

'How childish,' I said.

'Yes, and then there are all kinds of warnings in red paint all over *The Oshun Oxtra*,' continued the Joxter, 'and I suppose he hasn't finished yet.'

He hadn't.

The Island Ghost pestered us all the week; every night became filled with owl-hoots and knocks and tables jumping around and breaking. And when he finally found a piece of chain in Hodgkins's tool chest and ratttled it for four hours at a stretch the situation became unbearable. We decided to invite the ghost to a secret council and talk some sense into him. So we nailed a message to the palm-wine tree:

Dear Island Ghost,

For obvious reasons a special Ghost Council will be held at this place on Tuesday before sunset. Members' complaints will be attended to. Bring no chains, please.

Board of the Royal Colony

'Since when are we royal?' asked the Muddler.

'Since I became Inventor to the King,' answered Hodgkins.

'I must ask mother to embroider crowns on all my undies,' said the Mymble's daughter.

'It was more fun to have an Outlaw Colony,' I said. 'I'm feeling royal anyway.'

The ghost replied in the afternoon, with red paint on parchment. (The parchment was found to be Hodgkins's old raincoat, nailed to the tree with the Mymble's daughter's breadknife.)

Hodgkins read the message aloud:

'The Hour of Fate is nearing. Tuesday, *but* at midnight, when the Hounds of Death are howling in the lonely wilderness! Vain creatures, hide your snouts in the cold earth that rings with the heavy tread of the Invisible! Your Fate is written in blood on the walls of the Chambers of Terror. I'll bring my chain if I like.

The Ghost, called the Horriblest.'

'Well,' said Hodgkins. 'Fate's a word he's fond of, I see, and capitals. Don't be afraid. And don't be too brave, either. Wouldn't be polite.'

The ghost greeted us punctually at twelve o'clock with three hollow howls and a green light (that lost its effect on account of our camp fire.)

'I have come!' said the ghost in his inimitable tones. 'Tremble, mortals, for the revenge of the forgotten bones!'

'Evening,' said the Joxter. '*You* haven't forgotten those bones, I hear. Whose are they? Why don't you bury them?'

'Now, now, Joxter,' said Hodgkins. 'Don't tease him. Dear ghost. Wouldn't you please let us have some sleep? Can't you move somewhere else for a while?'

'Everybody's accustomed to me,' said the ghost sadly. 'Not even Edward the Booble's scared any more.'

'I was!' said the Muddler. 'I'm still scared!'

'That's kind of you,' replied the ghost thankfully and hastened to add: 'The lost skeleton caravan's wailing in icy moonlight!'

'Listen,' Hodgkins said kindly. 'You don't seem to have the fun you ought to have. I'll speak to the King. Perhaps he could give you a territory of your own. What? Something with a good supply of phosphorus and tin cans?'

97

'And fog horns?' said the ghost a little hesitantly. 'Do you think you could find me a real skeleton?'

'Do my best,' said Hodgkins. 'By the way. Do you know the thread-and-resin trick?'

'No! Tell me!' said the ghost with interest.

'Quite simple,' said Hodgkins. 'You take a length of thick sewing cotton. Number twenty at least. Fasten it to the window-frame (of an enemy). Stand outside and rub the thread with a piece of resin.'

'And it produces a noise of horror?' asked the ghost happily.

'It does. And if you happen to have a tin tube and a pair of stilts . . .' Hodgkins continued.

'By my demon eye, you're a real friend,' said the ghost and curled up at his feet. 'Tin tube, did you say? I have one.'

Then Hodgkins sat half the night describing the most astonishing devices for frightening people. He drew the constructions in the sand. And at dawn the ghost was elected a member of the Royal Colony and officially named The Terror of Horror Island.

'Listen,' I said, 'I wonder if you'd care to lodge with me? You can have the drawing-room to yourself. Not that I'm afraid to live alone, but it's always safer to have someone in the house.'

'By all the Hounds of Hell,' the ghost began, paling with annoyance. But then he calmed down and replied: 'Well, thanks, that's kind of you.'

I made him a nice bed out of a packing-case that I painted black with a decoration of skulls and bones in pale green. His feeding bowl I marked 'Poison' (to the Muddler's great satisfaction).

'Most cosy,' said the ghost. 'Please don't mind if I rattle a little at midnight. It's a habit.'

'Not at all,' I said. 'But not more than five minutes, and please keep away from the meerschaum tram. It's valuable.'

'All right,' said the ghost. 'But I'll take a whole night out on Midsummer Night.'

CHAPTER 7

Describing the triumphant unveiling of the Amphibian and its sensational trial dive to the bottom of the sea.

A N D Midsummer Night came and went (at the Eve the Mymble gave birth to her smallest daughter and named her My, which means The-smallest-in-existence) and the trees blossomed, the blossoms changed into oranges, the oranges were eaten (mostly by the Joxter), and nobody ever found the time to write those Colony laws.

Sometimes Edward the Booble waded to our shores and bawled at us as he was wont to do. I invented one philosophical truth after the other. The Joxter did nothing special, but said he felt fine. The ghost had taken to knitting socks and scarfs. The click and rattle was good for his nerves, he said.

But one special day – a lonely day when I longed to go away round the world with the Hattifatteners – something happened.

Hodgkins called a meeting of the council. He had put on his captain's cap and a solemn expression. We understood that something important had taken place and waited in silence for him to speak.

'My old crew,' Hodgkins began in a funny voice. 'This is a great day. *The Oshun Oxtra* is now an Amphibian.'

'Really,' said the Mymble's daughter.

'Excuse me, a what?' asked the Muddler.

'The houseboat is rebuilt. Into an Amphibian,' Hodgkins explained. 'An Amphibian's a submarine. On wheels. With wings.'

'Triumph!' I cried. 'Hodgkins, you're famous now!'

'Well,' he said. 'Perhaps not famous. But satisfied.'

The trial flight took place the same afternoon. The former *Oshun Oxtra* was placed on a platform in front of the Autocrat's throne and covered with a red canvas.

'A black one's much more festive, I think,' said the Island Ghost clicking away at his knitting. 'Or even a thin veil, ashen pale as midnight fog. The shade of horror, you know.'

'What a prattler he is,' said the Mymble who had brought all her children to the event. 'Hullo, dearest daughter! Come and look at your latest brothers and sisters!'

'Mother dear,' said the Mymble's daughter, 'have you made new ones again! Please tell them that their sister is a Colonial Princess on her way to a trip around the moon in an Amphibian.'

The Mymble kiddies bobbed, nodded, and stared.

Hodgkins disappeared behind the canvas to inspect his invention for the last time. 'Ought to test the exhaust,' he

said. 'Something's the matter with the pipe. Joxter! Go aboard, will you, and switch on the big fan!'

After a while the big fan was heard to start.

Almost at once a lump of oatmeal porridge came flying out from the exhaust pipe and hit Hodgkins in the eye.

'Strange sight!' he said in some surprise.

The Mymble kiddies shouted ecstatically.

'Our breakfast porridge,' Hodgkins said reproachfully to the Muddler.

'Excuse me,' the Muddler replied. 'There was a little left over, but I'm definitely sure I put it in the teapot. *Not* in the exhaust pipe.'

'What's wrong?' asked the Autocrat. 'May We begin Our opening speech, or are you too busy to listen?'

'It's just my little My, I hear,' explained the Mymble

delightedly. 'Such a little personality already! Porridge in an exhaust pipe! What an idea!'

'Don't take it too seriously, madam,' Hodgkins said, a little stiffly.

'May We begin or may We not?' asked the King.

'Please, Your Majesty, go ahead,' I said.

The fog horn gave a long blast, the Hemulic Voluntary Brass Band stood at attention, and Daddy Jones climbed to his throne amid general cheering. When all was silent again he spoke:

'Dear foggy-headed subjects! The occasion calls for a few solemn words. Take a good look at Hodgkins. Our Royal Surprise Inventor! His latest and greatest invention is to be unveiled shortly and starting on its pioneer voyage over land, through the ocean deep, and in the air. Please keep this bold enterprise somewhere at the back of your fuzzy minds when you are hopping around and generally passing the time of day. We are still expecting great things of you, dearest muddle-heads. Try to spread a little honour and glory over Our kingdom in the future, and if you can't do that, then at least give the hero of the day the best of your cheers!'

The people cheered enthusiastically. The Hemulens started on Daddy Jones's favourite waltz, and amid a shower of roses and Japanese pearls Hodgkins went up to the platform and pulled the silk rope.

The canvas fell to the ground.

It was a great moment.

The Hemulic Band changed over to the Autocratical Anthem (with the refrain: 'Surprised, aren't you?') and the Mymble, always easily moved, cried floods of tears.

Hodgkins pulled at the peak of his cap and went aboard,

followed by the Royal Outlaw Colony (with roses and Japanese pearls still raining over us), and the remaining space in the former *Oshun Oxtra* was speedily filled with Mymble kiddies.

'Excuse me!' the Muddler suddenly cried and jumped back over the gangway. 'By heck, I daren't! Not in the air! I'll be sick again!' He rushed back and disappeared in the crowd.

And a moment later the Amphibian began to tremble. The engines droned, the door was closed and bolted, and then the ship took a sudden leap from the platform and sailed over the tree-tops in the Garden of Surprises.

'We're up! We're up!' the Joxter cried.

Yes, one moment we were up in the air, the next we skidded over the waves, ploughing up a splendid foam.

'Hold on now,' Hodgkins cried. 'We're going down.' He pulled a lever.

Suddenly the Amphibian was filled by green light and swarms of bubbles went dancing across the port-holes.

'We'll never come up,' said little My.

I pressed my snout against the cold glass and looked out into the sea.

Hodgkins had switched on a row of headlights and we moved through the green deep in a circle of light.

'Are all the fish in bed?' the Joxter asked.

'They're afraid,' said Hodgkins. 'Wait a bit.'

We waited. In a little while a little fish-child came

swimming out of the green dark into our light. He seemed to hesitate, then he came up to the Amphibian and sniffed at it with great interest.

He carried a small lantern on his nose.

'Why doesn't he light it?' the Mymble wondered.

'Perhaps his battery's dead,' Hodgkins said. 'There's another one!'

In a few minutes dozens of small fish were swarming around us. Then some young sea-serpents and a few mermaids appeared, and finally a big bespectacled fishing-frog thrust his nose at one of the port-holes.

'Are they dumb?' I asked.

'Just a moment,' Hodgkins replied and turned a knob on his special wireless. There was a crackle, and then we heard the fishing-frog speak.

'I'm of the definite opinion that this thing reminds me not a little of a whale,' the fishing-frog said in the circumstantial manner he had acquired in two hundred and ten years of lonely swimming.

'But what a funny diet he keeps,' said the small fish-child. 'Look at that pale snouted fish he's swallowed! He'll have bad dreams tonight.'

'Meaning you,' said the Joxter and gave me a friendly pat on the back. 'He thinks you're the strangest fish here.'

'Be quiet, the serpent's talking,' I said.

'I'd be surprised if this whale would ever get the time to digest it,' now said the serpent. 'Blazing with light, indeed. He'll be caught sooner or later.'

'One asks oneself with a certain apprehension whether it's a manifestation of stupidity or of defiance,' said the fishing-frog. 'Still, one has to admit that the effect is most pleasing to the eye. I'm afraid my glasses do not allow me really to appreciate the illumination. But as a law-abiding citizen one asks oneself also what his wattage might be.'

'What's he talking of?' the Mymble asked.

'They seem to have some kind of lighting regulation,' the Joxter said with a snort. 'Apparently you're not allowed even to light the lamps on your own snout.'

'Very sensible,' remarked the Island Ghost. 'The night of fate veiling the cemetery in black shrouds. Black wraiths flitting through the dark. Good idea.'

Indeed, each one of the sea-people carried a small unlit lantern. They now formed a dense crowd around the Amphibian and seemed to like our light.

'It can't last,' said a cod. 'The Sea-Hound's sure to come.'

The crowd moved uneasily and the smallest fishes disappeared.

'Where's he hunting tonight?' the serpent asked anxiously.

'I heard him in the western parts before nightfall,' replied a sea-spook. 'There was a porpoise carrying a light. He ate it, of course.'

'They're off,' I said. 'Something's scared them.'

'They'll eat us,' said little My.

'I'd better put the kiddies to bed,' remarked the Mymble. 'Hurry up, please!'

Her children formed a circle to help each other with the back buttons.

'Count yourselves tonight,' said the Mymble. 'This excitement's made me so tired.'

'Aren't you going to read to us?' the kiddies cried.

'Yes, of course,' said the Mymble.

'Where did we stop last time?'

The kiddies chorused: 'This-is-one-eyed-Bob's-san-
guinary-work-remarked-Inspector-Twiggs-pulling-a-three
-inch-nail-from-the-ear-of-the-corpse-it-must-have-hap-
pened.'

'I know, I know,' said the Mymble. 'Hurry into bed
now and we'll say your prayers first.'

Just then we caught sight of the Sea-Hound on the
starboard.

It looked so terrifying that Hodgkins switched off all
the lamps at once.

But his surprise was so great that he wasn't able to
handle the ship properly, and instead of rising to the sur-
face the Amphibian dived down like a stone to the bottom
of the sea and started to crawl forward on her caterpillar
chains.

The sea-weed brushed our sides and clawed at our portholes like ghastly fingers. In the silent dark we heard the panting of the Sea-Hound chasing us. Now his grey snout with the long drooping whiskers appeared, horribly lighted by his evil yellow eyes. They were like a couple of searchlights that found the Amphibian and held it . . .

'Under the covers, children!' the Mymble cried. 'Here he comes!'

There was a crash and a sickening wrench astern. The Sea-Hound had started with the rudder.

And then followed a terrible upheaval. The Amphibian suddenly rose tail upwards and was thrown over on its back, loose sea-weed whirled around us in the churning water, and the general rush and roar drowned our wild shouts. We were thrown head over heels, all the cupboards flew open, the crockery came crashing out and was mixed on the floor with oatmeal, rice and tea, kiddies' boots, wool, knitting needles, and the Joxter's tobacco. And from outside came a blood-curdling, tail-bristling howling and roaring.

Then all was silent.

Quite silent.

'Dearmedearmedearme,' said the Mymble. 'How many children have I left? Count them, dearest daughter!'

But before the Mymble's daughter had even begun her task we heard a well-known terrible voice that shouted: 'I see! Here you are, you dish-rags! By all that's grokely! Did you think you could give me the slip, what? Always forgetting to tell me where you're going, aren't you?'

'Who's that, now?' the Mymble asked.

'I'll give you three guesses,' said the Joxter.

And Edward the Booble thrust his head under water and looked in at us through a port-hole. We looked back at him as composedly as possible, and then we noticed a few small pieces of Sea-Hound floating about: a bit of tail and a bit of whisker and some flat pieces. Because Edward the Booble had happened to tread on him.

'Edward! My true friend!' Hodgkins cried.

'We'll never forget this! You saved us at the last moment!' I said.

'Give the kind gentleman a kiss, kiddies,' said the Mymble and started to cry.

'What's that?' Edward the Booble said. 'No kiddies, please. They always get in my ears. You gnats! I've stubbed my toes looking for you everywhere, and you're talking through your hats as usual.'

'You've trod on the Sea-Hound!' the Joxter cried.

'Eh?' said the Booble and jumped back. 'Somebody again? Believe me, it wasn't my fault. And I really haven't the money for any more funerals . . .'

He continued angrily: 'Anyway, why don't you keep

your old dogs out of harm's way! I simply refuse to pay for it.'

And Edward the Booble went wading away. He looked deeply hurt. After a while he turned round and shouted: 'I'm coming for tea in the morning. And make it strong!'

Suddenly something happened.

All the sea lit up.

'We're burning,' said little My.

A million billion fishes came swimming from everywhere with blazing lanterns, pocket lights, searchlights, bull's-eyes, bulbs and acetylene lamps. The fishing-frog carried a bracket lamp in each ear, and everybody cheered like mad.

The bleak sea became illuminated with purple, red, and chrome-yellow sea anemones, and the serpents wheeled and turned somersaults.

We sailed home in triumph, criss-crossing over the Ocean, and we never quite knew whether the lights that shone through our port-holes were stars or fishes. Toward morning we sighted our island again, and by then most of us felt rather sleepy.

CHAPTER 8

In which I give an account of the circumstances of the Muddler's wedding, further touch on the dramatic night when I first met Moominmamma, and finally write the remarkable closing words of my Memoirs.

T E N miles (nautical) off the coast we sighted a dinghy carrying a signal of distress.

'It's the Autocrat,' I said in shocked tones. 'Do you think there can have been a revolution so early in the morning?'

'Revolution?' Hodgkins said and changed to full speed ahead. 'I hope my nephew's safe.'

'What's up?' the Mymble shouted when we reached the dinghy and it drew alongside.

'Up? Up!' Daddy Jones replied irritably. 'Everything's up. I mean, wrong. You'll have to come home at once.'

'Have the forgotten bones extracted their revenge at last?' asked the Island Ghost hopefully.

'It's your Muddler again,' the Autocrat panted as he climbed aboard. 'Take care of the dinghy, somebody! We came out to meet you Ourselves because We don't trust any of Our subjects.'

'The Muddler?' exclaimed the Joxter.

'Exactly,' replied the Autocrat. 'Of course We have nothing whatever against the marriage, but We won't stand for seven thousand Niblings and a savage Aunt in Our kingdom.'

'Who's marrying?' the Mymble asked.

'The Muddler, silly,' replied the Autocrat.

'Impossible,' Hodgkins said.

'Impossible or not, the wedding's today,' Daddy Jones answered.

'Who's the girl?' I cried, unable to hide my surprise.

'A Fuzzy,' said the King. 'Full speed ahead, please! Well, they fell head over heels in love at first sight, and they've been swapping buttons and running about holding hands and being generally silly ever since, and now they've sent a telegram to an aunt (but the Muddler says she's possibly eaten) and to seven thousand Niblings and invited them all to the wedding. And of course Our kingdom's in grave danger. The Niblings eat anything! Give Us a glass of wine, please!'

'Could it be that they've invited the Hemulen Aunt?' I asked, greatly shocked, and handed the Autocrat his drink.

'I suppose so,' he replied. 'An aunt with only half a snout and ill-tempered into the bargain. We are all for surprises but We like to make them Ourselves.'

We were nearing the coast.

At the end of the pier the Muddler was standing with the Fuzzy at his side.

'Well?' Hodgkins said and put in at the pier.

'Excuse me!' the Muddler cried. 'I'm married!'

'Me too!' the Fuzzy said and dropped a curtsey.

'But We told you to wait until the afternoon, didn't We?' exclaimed the Autocrat. 'Now you've spoiled the big wedding party!'

'Excuse us, please, we couldn't wait,' said the Muddler. 'We're so much in love!'

'Oh dear me, dear me!' cried the Mymble and rushed over the gangway. 'The best of luck to you both! What a sweet little Fuzzy! Give them three cheers, kiddies, they're married already!'

'They're past helping now,' said little My.

*

At this point Moominpappa was cut short by Sniff who sat up in his bed and cried: 'Stop!'

'Father's reading about his youth,' said Moomintroll reproachingly.

'And about *my* daddy's youth,' replied Sniff with unexpected dignity. 'I've heard a lot about the Muddler so far. But this is the first time I have heard about a Fuzzy!'

'I've forgotten to tell you,' said Moominpappa unhappily.

'You forgot my *mother*!' Sniff cried.

The door to the bedroom opened and Moominmamma looked in.

'Still awake?' she said. 'Did I hear somebody cry for mother?'

'It was me,' Sniff said and jumped out of his bed. 'Just think of it! Here we've heard lots and lots about daddies, and then suddenly one learns that one has had a mother as well!'

'But that's natural, isn't it?' replied Moominmamma blandly. 'Aren't you glad to learn it, Sniff?'

'Glad?' Sniff said and stopped in the middle of the floor. His frown disappeared. He stared at Moominpappa and suddenly he cried: 'Of course I'm happy! Did she have a button collection too?'

'She had,' Moominpappa said.

'A moment, please,' said Snufkin. 'Did I possibly have a—er—mother also?'

'Yes, yes, of course,' exclaimed Moominpappa. 'I was just coming to it. Dear me, yes. The Mymble, of course!'

'Then little My's my sister,' Snufkin said wonderingly.

'Certainly, certainly,' replied Moominpappa. 'But dearest children, please let me finish this chapter. Still, they're *my* memoirs, you know, and I'm not very keen on genealogy.'

'May he?' Moomintroll asked.

'Well,' Sniff and Snufkin consented.

'Thanks,' said Moominpappa and continued his reading.

*

The Muddler and the Fuzzy received wedding presents all through the day. At last the coffee tin was filled to the brim, and the rest of the buttons, stones, shells, door-knobs, and other things (too many to enumerate) had to be heaped beside it.

The happy couple sat holding hands on the heap. 'It's grand to be married,' the Muddler exclaimed.

'Possibly,' Hodgkins remarked. 'But listen, please. Just a detail. Why did you invite the Hemulen Aunt? And why the Niblings?'

'Excuse me, but I was so afraid to hurt their feelings,' the Muddler said.

'But the aunt?' I cried.

'Well,' answered the Muddler, 'to be frank I haven't missed her terribly. But excuse me! I've such a guilty conscience! Remember I wished somebody would be kind enough to eat her?'

'Mphm,' Hodgkins said. 'Yes. I see.'

On the following day, when the packet boat was due to arrive, the pier, the hills, and the beaches were thronged with the Autocrat's subjects. Daddy Jones's throne was placed on the highest hill, and the Hemulic Brass Band were polishing their instruments.

The Muddler and the Fuzzy sat holding hands in a special wedding boat, designed as a swan.

Everybody was feeling excited and a little uneasy, because the rumours of the Hemulen Aunt's energy and terrific sense of duty had spread like wild-fire over the kingdom. And moreover everybody wondered if the Niblings would undermine the country and gnaw the woods to pieces. But nobody said a word about their apprehensions to the newly-wedded couple who sat peacefully sorting buttons in their boat.

'Perhaps she could be scared off with thread and resin?' asked the Island Ghost. He was embroidering skulls on a teacosy for the Fuzzy.

'Not she,' I replied.

'We'll have a multiplication contest before evening,' the Joxter prophesied. 'And very possibly she'll remain over winter and make us *ski*!'

'What's that?' the Mymble's daughter asked.

'It's a way of overcoming the friction of atmospheric precipitation,' Hodgkins explained.

'Dear me,' the Mymble said.

'We'll die of it,' said little My.

A great shout rose from the crowd.

The packet boat was coming nearer.

The Hemulic Band launched into the anthem 'Save Our Silly People' and the wedding swan put out to sea. Two Mymble kiddies fell into the water from pure excitement, the fog horns blared, and the Joxter lost his nerve and fled.

Only then we noticed that the packet boat was empty, and it dawned upon us that it couldn't have held as many as seven thousand Niblings. Cries of relief mixed with disappointment were heard along the beach.

One single little Nibling jumped down in the wedding swan that now turned back towards the quay.

"What's this?' the Autocrat said. He hadn't been able to remain on his throne. 'Another party's spoiled! One single Nibling!'

'It's our own old Nibling,' I said. 'He's carrying a big parcel.'

'So she was eaten after all,' Hodgkins said.

'Silence! Silence! Silence!' shouted Daddy Jones and blew his pocket fog horn. 'Make way for the Nibling ambassador!'

The crowd made room for the bridal couple and the Nibling who shyly waddled up to us and laid his parcel on the ground. The edges and corners were slightly gnawed but in good condition.

'Well?' said the Autocrat.

'The Hemulen Aunt sends her compliments ...' said the Nibling, wildly searching his pockets.

Everybody jumped with impatience.

'Hurry, please,' said the King.

Finally the Nibling found a crumpled letter, straightened it out and began laboriously to read as follows:

'Dear Children,
It is with the deepest regret, with a guilty conscience and a feeling of having failed in my Duty, that I write you this letter. I am really not able to come to your wedding, and I understand that I can hardly hope for your forgiveness. Believe me, I felt happy and quite flattered to hear that you longed to see me again, and I have shed torrents of happy tears, I was so moved to hear about the little Muddler's decision to take one

of the most serious steps there are in life. Dear children, I really do not know how to thank you, first that you saved me from the Groke, and secondly that you acquainted me with the delightful Niblings. It is my Duty to tell you the bare truth: the Niblings and I have such fun together that not even a wedding party can draw us away from home. We are holding quizzes and multiplication contests every day for several hours at a stretch, and we are expectantly looking forward to the winter with its healthy exercise in the snow. To console you in your disappointment, I am, however, sending you a valuable wedding present, and hope it shall find a permanent place in the Muddler's tin.

With 6,999 greetings from my friends!

Yours very, very gratefully,

Hemulen Aunt.'

There was a long silence when the Nibling had finished.

'Do you like multiplication?' Hodgkins asked cautiously.

'Enormously!' replied the Nibling.

I sat down and didn't know what to say.

'Open it, please!' the Muddler cried.

The Nibling solemnly gnawed at the string and produced a full-size photograph of the Hemulen Aunt dressed as Nibling Queen.

'Her snout's all there!' the Muddler cried. 'I'm so glad!'

'Darling, look at the frame,' said the Fuzzy.

We all looked at the frame.

It was made of pure Spanish gold set with small roses of topaz and chrysolite in the corners. Small diamonds formed an inner fringe around the photograph. The back was all turquoises.

'Do you think they can be prised loose?' the Fuzzy asked.

'Surely!' replied the Muddler ecstatically. 'Didn't somebody give us a pricker?'

And at that moment a terrible voice was heard by the shore and it said: 'Well! You grokely dish-rags! I've waited and waited for my morning tea at the island, but not a soul seemed to remember old Uncle Edward!'

*

A couple of days after Moominpappa had read about the Muddler's wedding he was sitting on the verandah with his family. It was a windy August night. Moominmamma had made them some hot rum punch and treaclebread, and all were dressed in their very best and had combed their tails.

'Well?' asked Moominmamma expectantly.

'The Memoirs were finished today,' Moominpappa announced in a thick voice. 'At six-forty-five. And the closing sentence – it's – well, you'll hear.'

'Haven't you written anything about your wicked life with the Hattifatteners?' Snufkin asked.

'No,' replied Moominpappa. 'I want this to be an instructive book.'

'Exactly,' Sniff cried.

'Hush, hush,' Moominmamma said. 'But won't I come into the picture at all?' And she flushed pink.

Moominpappa took three large swigs from his glass and answered:

'You certainly do. Listen carefully, my son, because this last part tells of how I found your mother.'

*

Autumn came.

The gales began to howl around our lonely island and the weather was cold. All of us now lived in my house where there was naturally a good porcelain stove and where we intended to sleep through the winter.

The singular event I am about to relate took place one evening when the weather was really terrific.

The building creaked and groaned, the rain came rushing over the verandah roof with a patter like small running feet, and at times the roaring south-western gale puffed a little cloud of smoke back down

the chimney and out into the room where we sat in front of the fire.

'Please read to us, mother!' said the Mymble kiddies from their beds.

'Yes,' said the Mymble. 'Where did we stop?'

'Inspector-Twiggs-silently-crept-to-the-door,' the kiddies chorused.

'All right,' said the Mymble. 'Inspector Twiggs silently crept to the door. He was barely able to catch the gleam from a pistol in the moonlight. Coldly determined he advanced on the feet of Avenging Justice, stopped dead, and . . .'

Abstractedly I listened to the Mymble's tale. I had heard it many times.

'I like that story,' said the Island Ghost. He was embroidering a pen-wiper (crossbones on black flannel) while keeping an eye on the clock.

The Muddler and the Fuzzy sat nearest to the fire holding hands as usual.

It could hardly have been cosier. But I was intrigued by a strange and uneasy feeling.

Every now and then a gust of foam from the sea washed over the black and rattling window panes.

'To be out at sea on a night like this . . .' I said.

'A good hundred and fifty yards a second,' Hodgkins concurred.

'I'm going out for a breath of air,' I mumbled and opened one of the leeward doors.

For a moment I stood listening on the doorstep.

The dark night was filled with the menacing crash and tumble of the surf. I sniffed at the wind, turned back my ears and went over to the windward side.

The gale rushed at me with a devilish howl and I closed my eyes to avoid seeing all the fiendish things that are on the move on such nights. Things that are better ignored ...

I stumbled down to the beach that was made faintly visible by the gleaming edge of white foam. When the moon appeared through the flying clouds it made the wet sand shine like a metal disc. The sharp-edged waves came rolling in with a deafening roar, rose high with claws and fangs bared, crashed blindingly down and crept crackling and hissing back into the dark again.

My memories overcome me!

What made me defy the cold and the dark (that all

Moomins loathe) to struggle down to the beach at the exact moment when the sea carried Moomintroll's mother to our island?

Clinging to a spar she came shooting with the surf, was carried into the cove and sucked out again with the back-wash.

I rushed out in the water and shouted at the top of my voice: 'I'm here!'

She came back. She had lost hold of her spar and floated helplessly on her back with her legs in the air.

I did not bat an eyelid before the black wall of seething water. I caught the shipwrecked beauty in my arms, and the next second I was swept off my feet in the boiling surf.

With supermoominal strength I fought for a foothold – I managed to crawl ashore while the waves hungrily grabbed for my tail – and at last I laid my sweet burden on the beach, safe from the wild and cruel sea!

Oh, this was not in the least like rescuing the Hemulen Aunt! This was a Moomin, like myself, but still more beautiful, a little Moomin woman that I had saved!

Suddenly she sat up and cried:

'Save my handbag! Oh, save my handbag!'

'But you're holding it!' I answered.

'Oh, glory be!' she said. She opened her large black handbag and started rummaging in its depths. At last she found her powder compact.

'I'm afraid my powder's sea-damaged,' she said sadly.

'You're every bit as beautiful without it,' I replied gallantly.

She gave me an unfathomable look and blushed deeply.

*

Let me stop here, at this remarkable turning-point of my stormy youth, let me close my Memoirs at the moment when the most wonderful of Moomins comes into my life! Since then my follies have been supervised by her gentle and understanding eyes, and thereby transformed into sense and wisdom while losing little of the enchantment and liberty that have led me to write them down.

It is a terribly long time since all this happened, but when I have now related it anew to myself I have a decided feeling that it could all happen again, in some quite new manner.

I'm laying down my memoir-pen convinced that hundreds of new adventures await me, still greater, still more astonishing.

I would like every young Moomin to consider my exploits, my courage, my good sense, my virtues, and my follies – even if he would never be wiser from the experience he will one day have to acquire for himself in the wondrous way that is natural for all youthful and talented Moomins.

This is
THE END
of the Memoirs.

EPILOGUE

MOOMINPAPPA laid his memoir-pen on the verandah table and looked in silence at his family.

'Your health!' said Moominmamma with great emotion.

'Your health,' Moomintroll said. 'Now you're famous!'

'Eh?' said Moominpappa and jumped in his chair.

'When this book's published you're sure to be famous,'
said Moomintroll.

The author wiggled his ears and grinned.

'Perhaps!' he said.

Sniff cried: 'But then – what happened then?'

'Oh – then,' Moominpappa replied and made a vague
sweeping gesture that comprised the house, the family,
the garden, the Moomin Valley, and generally everything
that follows after one's youth.

'Dear children,' said Moominmamma shyly. 'Then
everything *started*.'

A sudden gust of wind rattled the windows.

'To be out at sea on a night like this ...' said Moominpappa abstractedly.

'What about *my* daddy?' Snufkin asked. 'The Joxter?
What became of him? And of mother?'

'Yes, and the Muddler?' asked Sniff. 'Did you lose the only daddy I ever had? Not to speak of his button collection and the Fuzzy?'

Moominpappa hesitated.

And at that exact moment, singularly enough, at the very moment needed for this story – there was a rap on the door.

Three hard, short knocks.

Moominpappa snatched his gun from the wall and cried: 'Who's there?'

A deep voice answered: 'Open the door, Moomin! The night is cold!'

Moominpappa let go of the gun and threw the door wide. '*Hodgkins!*' he cried.

Yes, in walked Hodgkins, shook the rain off himself and said:

'It took some time to find you. Hullo. You're not a day older.'

'Nor you either,' cried Moominpappa. 'Oh, what happiness! Oh, how glad I am!'

Then a small, hollow voice was heard to say: 'On a night of fate like this the forgotten bones rattle more than ever on the lonely beach!' And the Island Ghost climbed out of Hodgkins's knapsack with a friendly grin.

'Glad to meet you,' said Moominmamma. 'Would you like a glass of rum punch?'

'Thanks,' Hodgkins said. 'One for me. And a few for the others outside.'

'Have you brought somebody?' asked Moominpappa.

'Yes, a few parents,' Hodgkins replied.

'Whose parents?' shouted Sniff and Snufkin.

'Yours of course,' said Hodgkins. 'They're a little shy. Didn't want to come in with me.'

Sniff disappeared through the verandah door with a howl and came back hauling after him a wet and embarrassed Muddler holding hands tightly with a Fuzzy.

Behind them strolled the Joxter with an unlit pipe between his teeth, and last came the Mymble and the Mymble's daughter and thirty-four small Mymble kiddies. The verandah was filled to bursting point.

It was an indescribable night!

Never before has any verandah held so many questions, exclamations, embraces, explanations, and rum punches at the same time. And when the Muddler at last began to unpack his button collection and gave it away on the spot to his son, the feast reached its height. The Mymble began to collect her children and put them to bed in the cupboards.

'Silence!' cried Hodgkins and raised his glass. 'Tomorrow...'

'Tomorrow,' repeated Moominpappa with shining eyes.

'Tomorrow the adventures begin anew,' Hodgkins continued. 'Because I'm treating you all to a bit of travel. Everybody present. Mothers, daddies and kiddies. With the former *Oshun Oxtra*, the world's foremost Amphibian! Are you coming?'

'Not tomorrow, tonight!' shouted Moomintroll.

And in the foggy dawn they all tumbled out in the garden. The eastern sky was a wonderful rose-petal pink, promising a fine clear August day.

A new door to the Unbelievable, to the Possible, a new day that can always bring you anything if you have no objection to it.

I am Moominmamma.
Turn over and see
what Moominpappa
has to show you . . .

I am Moominpappa, but of course, you all know me by now. Here I am in pensive mood – I wish I knew where that hat disappeared to.

This is Sniff, one of Moomintroll's young friends. A little clumsy sometimes, but means well. After all the Muddler was his father.

A solitary chap, young Snufkin. Quite unlike the Joxter, his father, but with the same independent outlook on life.

I don't quite know what the Groke is doing here. She isn't much use for anything except as an exclamation!

Ha! here is the would-be-philosopher, our old friend the Muskrat, who likes to be left in peace to think – at least that is what he wants us to believe he is doing.

These two are apt to turn up anywhere. Thingummy and Bob – mischievous pair, too fond of pea-shooters and such; but I was young once.

The feminine touch. The Snork Maiden has taken a fancy to Moomintroll, but look what he did for her. Now I remember when I was a boy . . .

But to proceed. Moom-
introll – now there is a
chip off the old Moomin-
block if you like. An
eternal reminder of my
youth . . .

As for the Hemulen –
why do they wear so
much clothing? Must
remember to look that up
– he is our leading
Moominphilatelist a n d
also sound on Moomin-
chology.

So, if you want to read more about these curious but like-
able inhabitants of Moominland, you should look at the
list of books at the front. I wrote the notes above in 1952,
how time goes, and have now added a few more opposite.

Misabel we met that curious summer. How she enjoyed acting in my plays, and changing clothes.

A tremendous big fellow that Hemulen who invaded the valley one winter. One of those terrific do-gooders. Hmm – bit noisy.

Ah, Too-ticky – much addicted to bathing-houses, the sea-side in every particular in fact, and quite a philosopher in a way.

No selection would be complete without Little My. What would we do without her imperturbability – good word, what! good girl, good-bye for now.